BOOK 2 OF MORNA'S LEGACY SERIES

LOVE BEYOND REASON

A SCOTTISH TIME TRAVEL ROMANCE

BETHANY CLAIRE

Editor: Dee Pace & Dj Hendrickson
Cover Designer: Damonza
Formatting by RikHall.com

Available In eBook & Paperback

eBook ISBN: 978-0-9899502-5-1
Paperback ISBN: 978-0-9899502-2-0

http://www.bethanyclaire.com

For Maegan

Chapter 1

Three days I'd sat in the small room at the inn, only a short distance from the castle ruins. Surrounded by what were now considered artifacts of the castle, I took my time, spending days feigning illness so I could decide what I should do next.

Gwendolyn, the kind innkeeper, and her husband, Jerry, were growing impatient. I knew they wouldna allow me to stay in the room much longer without explanation, but what was I to tell them? I could hardly believe the truth myself.

With Adelle's help, I'd been able to fool the innkeepers into believing I was Adelle's daughter Bri, by remaining for the most part silent when interacting with them. With Adelle no longer here to speak for me, I knew they would notice my lack of an American accent.

A knock at the door meant 'twas evening, and Gwendolyn was bringing my supper. She'd graciously and unquestioningly brought each meal and left it outside the door since I'd arrived back at the inn claiming to be quite ill. She'd given me the privacy I'd so clearly desired, and so it surprised me to hear her speak from the other side of the door.

"I'm sorry to disturb your rest, but Jerry and I are both worried about you, dear. You've spent far too much time inside the room, so you've left me no choice I'm afraid. You can either clean yourself up and join us for dinner downstairs, or I shall be calling a doctor to come see to you at once."

Gwendolyn paused, waiting for my response. I wasna ill, only worried, and I wouldna have them send for a doctor for a non-existent sickness.

"Twill be...I'll be down shortly." A short response was best. Perhaps, my accent wouldna be as noticeable with only a few short words. Not that it mattered. I was going to have to tell them all I knew, not that they would believe me.

At this point, I had nothing left to lose.

* * *

I walked down the stairs and into the small kitchen to be met by kind smiles from both Gwendolyn and Jerry. The old man gave me a thorough look over before speaking bluntly, true to form.

"Ye must be feeling much better, lass. Ye doona look sick at all. Now sit down here and tell us where yer mother is. We know something has happened, and it is time that ye tell us what that is. Gwendolyn is too polite to ask ye, but I've no problem with tellin ye that yer behavior has been quite strange."

The old man stood to usher me to a chair across from both of them. Once I was seated, he resumed his place next to his wife. I sat silently for a moment, quite unsure of where to begin. I knew my accent would garner questions from them right away. "Aye, I'm no longer feeling ill, but I do need to tell ye both something."

Gwendolyn pinched her eyebrows together oddly in my direction. "Well, my goodness, Bri. I know it's tempting once you've been here awhile to try and speak like everyone around you, but I've never been very successful at it myself. You sound as if you've lived here forever."

Jerry laughed in response as he patted Gwendolyn on the shoulder. "Aye, my lassie's voice holds nothing of Scotland, although she's lived here for forty years now. She still speaks as if she arrived in the country only yesterday."

Gwendolyn leaned sweetly into Jerry before glancing back in my direction and continuing, "The accent really is great, but why are you doing it?"

I glanced down at me plate of untouched food, not quite ready for either of them to think I'd lost my mind.

Jerry reached across the table to gently squeeze my hand and, as I looked up at him, I could see the concern in his face. "Where's yer mother, lass?"

"She's no me mother. And I'm no Bri. I doona think ye will believe what I must tell ye, but will ye listen to all of it before ye decide that I'm mad?" I lifted my head to look them in the eye as I waited for their answer.

Jerry and Gwendolyn exchanged an unreadable sideways glance before Jerry spoke first. "Aye, lass. O'course we shall listen to ye. Let us move next to the fire though. The chairs in there are much more comfortable."

Gwendolyn simply nodded before they both stood and left me to follow them into the next room.

Once seated, I fumbled uneasily with my words, unsure of how to begin. One question had sat at the forefront of my mind since the first night I'd left Adelle at the castle ruins. I'd been too afraid to ask, for if the answer was not what I hoped, it meant everyone I'd known and loved had died only days ago, unable to change history. I knew that I must learn the truth before I explained anything further to Jerry and Gwendolyn.

"Might I ask ye a question before I tell ye?" I dinna wait for their response. "The castle ruins, I suppose they're still ruins, aye?"

Hope fluttered in my chest at the quizzical looks by both Jerry and Gwendolyn.

Jerry pointed in the direction of the castle. "Do ye mean Conall Castle, lass? If so, I wouldna go calling the place a ruin. It's still beautifully intact. A fine structure and a popular visit for tourists."

I was unsure of what a "tourist" was, but if what he said was true, it meant that they'd been successful at stopping the attack. Adelle, Bri, Eoin, Mary, Arran, had most likely all gone on to live for many more years. That knowledge was enough to rid myself of any other fears I had about moving on in this time alone.

"Do ye really mean it? The castle is no just a pile of rocks? It wasna destroyed long ago?" I needed just one more reassurance in order to let myself fully believe him.

Gwendolyn nodded and spoke this time. "Yes, dear. The Conalls have been one of the most powerful and beloved clans in Scotland for centuries. Descendants still own the castle, but they've partnered with the historical society to open it up for visitors. Are you sure you're still not ill?"

I nodded, relieved beyond explanation. It was time to explain to them what had happened. Then regardless of their reaction, it was time for me to move on from this place and start a new life here on my own.

"Aye, I feel fine. But I need to tell ye what's happened, and 'tis a long story. I doubt that ye will believe me."

Jerry smiled and sat back in his chair, settling in. "Why doona ye just get on with it, lass? Then we will decide what we believe."

"Aye. I'm no sure of where to begin. The first thing I should tell ye is that I'm no Bri. My name is Blaire MacChristy. My father was laird of MacChristy Castle during the seventeenth century. I was betrothed to Alasdair Conall's eldest son, Eoin, but on the day of our wedding in the year sixteen hundred and forty-five, I found meself swept up by a spell cast by Alasdair's late sister, Morna Conall, a witch who died when I was verra young. As ye can see, Bri and I look verra much the same with our hair dark and our eyes blue, and Morna knew that we would. She cast the spell so that if Bri and I ever laid eyes on the same spelled plaque in a spell room beneath the castle, we would switch places in time. Nearly two months ago, her spell worked. Bri was sent back and I was brought forward." I paused to look up at them and was surprised to see that they both seemed rather unsurprised by my words.

Instead, Jerry asked a question as if we were having the most normal of conversations. "Lass, why did Morna want ye to switch places? And where is Adelle?"

It took me a moment to speak. Was it possible that he believed what I was saying? "Ye see, that's why I asked ye if the castle was ruins. When I arrived here, it was. When Adelle and Bri came here, it was in ruins. Only a few short months after me wedding, the Conalls were murdered and the castle destroyed. No one ever found out who murdered them and that was why Bri and Adelle came to Scotland, to search for something that might reveal who had murdered the Conalls. Tis for the same reason that Morna cast the spell. She hoped that if Bri and I switched places, Bri's knowledge of what was to come would enable her to stop it. And she did. If no, then the castle would still be in ruins now."

5

"And Adelle?" Jerry continued to stare at me as if he wasn't shocked by my story.

"Once Adelle realized that we'd been switched, we spent weeks searching for a spell that could switch us back. We found one, but Bri dinna want to return. She married Eoin, and they fell in love. I dinna want to go back either, there's no much left for me there." I paused as an uncomfortable knot lodged itself in my chest. I swallowed hard, pushing it down, and continued. "Adelle wanted to be with Bri. So she did the spell instead, and it worked. She's with Bri now. 'Twas three days ago when I arrived here alone telling ye I was sick. I dinna know what to do." I leaned back in my own chair and crossed my hands in my lap.

Gwendolyn had remained silent when Jerry had spoken up, and I could tell nothing by her face.

The three of us sat in silence for what seemed like much longer than I'm sure it was. Eventually, Gwendolyn stood and walked to the other side of the room behind me and reached up to the top of the bookshelf lining the wall and pulled a small box from the shelf.

She returned to her seat next to Jerry and smiled at him quickly before extending the box in my direction. "I'd like to tell you a story myself if you don't mind, dear."

Confused, I only nodded and took the box to sit it in my own lap.

Gwendolyn pointed at the box. "Open it, and pull out the top three photographs."

I obeyed, lifting the small metal latch that kept the lid closed and looked down inside the box. I remembered the first time I'd seen a photograph, the first day I'd arrived in this time. Adelle had shown me one of Bri to emphasize just how much we resembled

6

one another. Despite all the strange and wonderful things I'd seen, it was still miraculous to me that moments could be captured forever on a small piece of parchment.

Only three photographs lay inside, all facing down, and I lifted them out and closed the lid before turning them over. As I did, the air around me chilled suddenly as I gazed at the images.

The first was of Conall Castle, but not as I remembered it. It was the castle in ruins as it had been when I arrived in this time.

The second was of the spelled plaque, still painted with my portrait, staring back at me. A reminder of the day my life had changed forever.

The first two images were shocking, but it was the third that caused my hands to shake and my breath to come out unsteadily as I glanced up at Gwendolyn. She only smiled softly, waiting for me to speak.

The third photograph was less a picture and more of a painted portrait, depicting people I'd known in my old life. Alasdair, young and vibrant, holding a baby Arran in his arms, while Eoin, no more than five, stood next to his father, only knee high. Alasdair's other arm was draped around a woman's shoulder, squeezing her tightly with affection. The woman was not Alasdair's late wife. She'd died giving birth to Arran, and I knew there was only one other person the woman could be. The witch, Morna.

While her face in the portrait was younger, it matched Gwendolyn's exactly.

* * *

Gwendolyn eventually gave up on waiting for me to respond. Laughing heartily, she reached out and squeezed me hand. "Come, dear. Surely after all you've been through, nothing can be too much of a surprise to you."

I looked over at Jerry who only nodded in confirmation. "Do ye mean? How could ye be her? She died when I was a verra small child."

"There are a far manner of things, dear, that seem impossible. Surely this is no more impossible than you sitting here in this century when you were born in another, aye?"

Gwendolyn slowly lost the American accent she'd been using the entire time I'd known her. She was right. After all I'd been through, I had no trouble believing her, but I dinna understand why.

"If ye could end up here after yer own death, then why would ye bother with the spell for me and Bri? Could ye no have stopped the massacre yerself?"

Gwendolyn, or Morna, I wasna sure which name was now appropriate, smiled as if expecting my question.

"Because, lass, there are more important things than life and death. Me spell put into motion other things just as important as saving the lives of me family members. Souls needed to meet. Souls that belonged together, despite being born centuries apart. Without me spell, that could never have been."

"Do ye mean Eoin and Bri?" Looking at her more closely, I noticed a resemblance to Alasdair, Eoin, and Arran that I'd never seen before. The shape of their eyes, the slant of their smiles, all strong Conall traits that made me trust her story even more.

"Aye. Eoin and Bri. Not to mention, there was me own lad, who dinna exist in me own time. Instead of saving me family meself, I chose to sit back and watch over those who would save them, while at the same time finding the man I was meant to love."

"Ye mean, Jerry isna like ye?"

8

Jerry cackled and coughed before he spoke. "Oh no, lassie! I was born right here, in this time and if I had the gift of magic like her, I'd have stopped me knees from cracking long ago."

Morna frowned in Jerry's direction. "I've told ye before, I could stop it for ye meself, but ye willna let me." She turned toward me once more. "He accepts the truth, but it all still makes him a wee bit uncomfortable. He willna let me use magic on him."

"So ye mean ye knew I wasna Bri?"

"Aye, lass. But I'll tell ye, I dinna expect ye to stay here and Adelle to go back. Me visions dinna show me that. Perhaps they dinna want me to try and stop it from happening. Are ye certain that ye wish to stay here?"

Panic shot through me at the thought of going back. I answered too quickly, startling both Morna and Jerry. "Aye! I canna go back."

Morna's face softened, her eyes showing that she understood. "All right, lass. Well, what is it that ye want to do now? We shall help ye get settled wherever ye'd like to go. Do ye wish to stay in Scotland?"

I'd given it no thought. I'd been too concerned with what I was going to tell them and whether or not Adelle and Bri had been able to stop the massacre to think much further into my future than a few moments. "I'm no sure. I doona know what to do."

Jerry leaned over and squeezed my hand, and there was no doubt in my mind that Morna had chosen well. Her husband was the best of men, kind to his core.

Morna waved a hand in the air as if dismissing my concern. "Doona worry. Why doona we help ye get settled in Edinburgh? We could get ye a job and a place to stay, and ye can see how ye like it for a while. If ye decide later that ye'd like to go elsewhere, then we'll be more than happy to help ye."

"Aye, that will be fine. Thank ye. I suppose ye shall be glad to have another empty room for guests, aye?"

Morna stood and motioned for me to do the same as we made our way to the stairs. Clearly, we were all about to retire for the evening.

"Lass, we doona allow other guests. Ye are the only one who knows this house is here. Only yerself and those I wish to see it can see this house along the side of the road. We'd be overrun with tourists, otherwise."

Chapter 2

Conall Castle – Scotland – 1646

Arran Conall made his way down to the stables for his daily ride. The remaining men of what was formerly the Kinnaird Clan remained camped out on the castle grounds, nearly two months after the demise of the clan's wretched laird.

Laird Kinnaird had given birth to no sons and, with his daughter still unmarried, the clan remained at Conall Castle under his brother's blessing while they tried to sort out a way to name their next leader.

Arran found himself stifled, standing in an open field. Now, with guests tucked into every free corner of the castle and its grounds, his daily work and rides in the stables were all that kept him from insanity.

He needed to keep busy anyway. The loss of his beloved Blaire to a century beyond his comprehension occupied his thoughts every moment. He was happy that his brother had found love in his new wife, Bri, but with her face so similar to Blaire's, it only reminded him of his own heartache every time he laid eyes on his new sister-in-law.

If he'd known his rejection of Blaire would have sent her so far from him, he would have defied his brother and never let her go. He would live with the regret of hurting her for the rest of his life.

Arran shook his head, doing his best to shake all thoughts of his beloved from his conscious mind. He saw enough of her in his dreams. It was torture to see her in the recesses of his mind when he was awake as well.

Rounding the corner of the entrance to the stables, he found Edana Kinnaird, the daughter of the late, villainous laird, feeding an apple to his brother's old horse, Griffin. The stables were usually occupied by only the castle's fleet of horses along with the old stable master, Kip. But Arran was surprised to find that his spirits lifted at the sight of his new friend.

While many women and children of Kinnaird's clan had stayed inside the castle, Edana was the only one who had her own room upstairs along with members of the family. For the past months, Edana had stayed in his late mother's room just down the hall from his own. He saw her often, and although she always kept their conversations short, he could tell by the way she watched him that she fancied him.

He could never return her feelings, his own heart swept away to a different time with another lass. If he'd met Edana only a year ago, he'd have already tupped her repeatedly and tossed her aside without so much as another thought. But Blaire had changed him irreparably, and it caused him to look at Edana's feelings toward him in a kinder light. He liked the lass, and he respected her. He wanted to do all he could to show her friendship.

She'd been through much as a child, living with her brute of a father, who Arran was certain had abused the young girl physically, and mayhap even in more unthinkable ways as well. From what he could see, she was a kindhearted lass, and with all her family gone, he knew she must be terrified over the uncertainty of her own future.

Smiling wide, he made his way toward her, reaching up to rub Griffin behind his ears.

"Ah, Griffin. Ye sure are a lucky lad today, are ye no? I'm sure ye are glad to be receiving such a treat from a lady rather than me or Kip, aye?" Arran winked at Edana and turned to address her. "Ye shall spoil him, lass. I fear he shall never take an apple from me again. He'll always want to eat it out of yer delicate hands."

Edana blushed, and Arran didn't miss how she averted her eyes from him before speaking.

"Nay, I doubt it. He doesna seem too particular about who's giving him the treat. He only wants to eat the apple."

"I doona know about that. I canna think of a time I've seen him look so pleased. What are ye doing down here? I doona believe I've seen ye here before." Arran continued to stroke Griffin, hoping that if he looked distracted with the horse, it would ease Edana's nerves.

"I'm grateful that ye and yer brother have allowed me to stay here. Lady Bri is exceedingly kind, but I tire of being indoors, and I canna stand to hear the men speak any further about how they shall replace me father."

Edana's brow creased in a pained expression, and Arran reached forward to place a hand on her shoulder to comfort her. She jerked away from him as if touched by fire, and Arran quickly went back to stroking Griffin. "I doona blame ye for needing to get away, but doona be worried about yer clan, lass. No matter who takes over as laird, ye shall no lose yer place in the castle. I promise that I'll see that ye are provided for just as ye have always been."

13

Arran glanced quickly in Edana's direction as she fumbled with her hands nervously, obviously unsure of how to respond. He dinna press her and turned to see to the other horses. As he walked away, she finally spoke again.

"Thank ye, Arran. I doona deserve yer kindness. I'm no so good as I believe ye think that I am."

Arran stopped walking and spun to face Edana once more. "Doona talk in that manner, lass. Ye deserve every kindness in the world." He paused, deciding that he could attend to the stables later. Perhaps what the lass needed most was to be left alone. "Now, I'll leave ye in peace. Spend as much time with the horses as ye wish. If ye decide ye would like to go for a ride, Kip would be more than happy to assist ye."

Smiling briefly, he turned and left. Perhaps it was time he talked to his brother about their guests. They needed to choose a leader and then return back to their own castle and territory. He dinna like to see Edana so distressed. The least he could do for her was to see her safely settled.

* * *

Edana Kinnaird watched until she was sure Arran was out of sight. Shivering beneath her clothes, she reached up to brush her shoulder harshly where he'd touched her. She could scrub the spot all day, and it would never be enough to rid herself of the Conall filth that he'd now placed there.

She couldn't stand another moment in captivity here. Each day she spent with the ever-kind and polite Conalls made her hate them that much more.

Her father had been a horrible man. Violent, angry, and disgusting, he'd beaten her mother's spirit until she'd died of sadness. He'd spent much of his life trying to do the same to Edana. But she was far stronger than her mother. At least her father had even admitted that much.

Edana had always hated her father as well, but he was all she'd had in the world, and she would never be able to forgive the family responsible for his death. Edana had even gone to the Conalls before her father's planned attack, warning them that he planned to murder them. She'd tried to do the right thing, but it had cost her everything.

Despite Arran's well-intentioned promises, she knew that as soon as a leader rose up among the cowardly men of her father's clan, she would lose her place as lady of the keep. The new laird would marry, and Edana would be cast out, hated for her father's crimes.

She'd learned enough of manipulation from her father to know that she had Arran just where she wanted him. With each quick glance away from him and each blush of her cheeks, she knew he thought she cared for him. It would make him weak, as love does to all people, and then she would be in the perfect position to avenge her father's death.

With each bat of her lashes in Arran's direction, the desperate seed of revenge took root, twisting its way through every last corner of her mind as she worked out a way to continue her father's work and destroy the Conalls.

She'd failed her father once by giving away his plan, she would not disappoint him again.

Chapter 3

"Just stay still for a minute, Mom. Can't you tell I'm trying to talk to you about something?" Bri reached a hand out to grab onto the side of her mother's dress, hoping it would deter her from continuing the raid on her closet. A habit her mother had developed in the twenty-first century remained even today when all she owned was a handful of dresses. Her mother still enjoyed stealing her clothes.

"Do you think I could talk Mary into making a few more gowns for me? She does such lovely work."

Bri watched as her mother turned and joined her at the end of the bed. Quickly hiking up her dress, Adelle kicked off her shoes and jumped up onto the feathered ticking so that she sat cross-legged facing Bri. Both women, while now considered beloved members of the family, stood out as oddities in this century. Their relaxed social manners and American accents branded them as the foreigners they were.

Bri smiled, amazed at her mother's vanity when they now lived in a place where mirrors were few and far between, and just the fact that they had all their teeth set them apart as rare beauties. "I'm sure she would, but I'd expect she will have you chipping in on a lot of the work."

Adelle laughed. "Oh yes, I expect that she will. Now, what is it that you were wanting to talk about?"

"Blaire." Bri paused, knowing that the mention of her look-alike would cause a reaction from her mother.

"Oh. Why? I miss the sweet girl terribly, but there's nothing I can do for her here except hope and pray that she's happy and has adjusted well."

Bri watched as her mother's eyes shifted downward, an odd occurrence for such a forthright woman and a sure sign she truly was heartsick over the idea of Blaire being left in the twenty-first century all alone.

"Well, maybe there is something we can do. I've been spending a lot of time in the spell room—"

Bri was cut off as her mother interrupted her, her mother's voice shrill and panicked. "What? Bri, you have no business ever entering that room again. It's already taken you from me once. Besides, I like it here. I don't want to have to follow you back if it sucks you back through time again."

Bri rolled her eyes at the expected melodramatics. "It isn't just a big wormhole that's going to suck me in with some sort of magnetic pull. It's all based on Morna's spells. And there are others that can work, that could bring us back and forth as we please. I'm sure there are risks, but I think that they might be worth taking."

"What for? I didn't keep Blaire from returning here, Bri. She suggested that I go in her place. She didn't want to come back here. She chose to stay."

Bri nodded. "I know all that, but why did she not want to come back? Did she ever tell you? I think she was heartbroken."

Adelle's face blanched and her eyes widened with surprise. "She never spoke of it, but I think you might be right. She said that there was no longer anything here for her, as if she lost something dear."

17

"Have you noticed the way Arran avoids me at almost all cost? When we do run into each other, the look in his eyes breaks my heart. Did I ever tell you about what happened with Arran?" Bri smiled as she watched the color spread to her mother's face once more, the anticipation of a juicy story exciting her mother immediately just as Bri knew that it would.

"No, I've never noticed. And no, you never told me! But, I expect you to right this instant."

"The night of my wedding to Eoin, Arran came to our bedchamber door thinking it was his own. He was very drunk. Anyway, Eoin was helping put out a small fire at the reception, so I had to help Arran down to his own room. To make a long story short, he kissed me. Granted, he thought I was Blaire, but it was clear that the two of them had been involved. And he loved her very much." Bri readjusted herself on the edge of the bed, reaching for a cushion to prop herself up more comfortably while she waited for her mother's response.

"Oh, wow. So you're telling me that you've kissed both of them?" Adelle paused and waved her hand in the air in dismissal. "Never mind, that's beside the point. But you know, I do remember that Arran seemed upset the day I arrived and told you that Blaire chose to stay."

"Yes he was, and I'm worried about him. Each day he drinks a little more than he did the day before. He's broken. I want to go and talk to Blaire, let her know that Arran is still in love with her and see if she would want to come back. Do you think that she would, Mom?" Bri sat patiently while her mother thought about the question. Finally, Adelle looked up and into Bri's eyes.

"I don't know, honey. She was very private. The two of you may look alike, but you are quite different. She was curious about

18

modern things and did her best to keep conversation on that. She didn't ever want to talk about herself."

Bri shifted uncomfortably, her resolve on her decision to meddle shaky. "Do you think it would be a pointless effort? There is another reason why I'd like to go back as well—some unfinished business that I feel I must take care of."

Adelle's eyebrows rose, nearly reaching the top of her hairline. "What's that, dear?"

"Several things actually. School, Mitsy, and to put an end to the missing persons report I'm certain Mitsy has filed. I need to go clear things up with her and stop whatever police departments are searching for me."

"They won't be searching for you. While Blaire and I were at the inn, the police called searching for you. I instructed Gwendolyn and Jerry to tell them you were fine but did not wish to speak to them. I called the station back later pretending to be you so they'd close the missing persons report. I also falsified reports from the dig and scheduled them to be sent out at different intervals for the next three months. Most likely, the grant committee is just now starting to realize that something is off."

"Well, that's good to know. I'm glad my disappearance didn't make national news."

"Are you sure you want to do this? Eoin will never let you go."

"Eoin isn't going to keep me from going anywhere. I'm sure he will be against it, but it's something I must do. Arran needs her, and Mitsy needs to know what happened to me. It's only weeks until her wedding. I won't have her worry over me ruin her big day."

Adelle stood, and Bri remained on the bed as her mother made her way to the bedchamber door. "Well, I know you will do what you feel is right. Good luck telling this to Eoin. You are far braver than I."

*   *   *

Austin, TX – Present Day

"Look. I didn't come here to ask your permission, Principal Hendricks. I've already booked the flight. You can either approve the days, or I'll quit. But either way, I'm going to Scotland to look for Bri. I'm only asking to leave a week earlier than I was originally scheduled for my wedding anyway. The substitute has been here for months now. She doesn't need me in the classroom with her. Now, are you going to sign off on it, or do I need to submit my resignation?"

Mitsy soon-to-be Fredrickson stood across the desk from the twin of Mr. Clean, who was Principal Hendricks. She stood with her arms crossed firmly across her chest as she tapped her foot in his direction.

Principal Hendricks crossed his own arms and looked her up and down as if gauging the seriousness of her words. "You know that the police have already closed the case, Mitsy, and we've already terminated her contract here with the district. The police chief told you himself that they have confirmation in Scotland that Bri is unharmed and still in the country. Ms. Montgomery did this to herself. Why do you feel the need to seek her out?"

Mitsy's head pounded as her blood pressure rose. When she spoke, she found that her voice came out more as a scream than intended but, once released, she couldn't rein it in. "Because some old innkeeper telling the police that the girl they've described is staying with them is not confirmation that she's all right. Neither is them speaking to someone who is supposedly Bri on the phone. The innkeepers said she wouldn't take my calls. She wouldn't do that. She knows me, and she knows how worried I'd be. For Christ's sake, the couple the police talked to could have murdered her!" Mitsy sat down in the chair opposite Principal Hendricks, her legs shaky and unsteady.

"The police also contacted the archaeological society that Bri's mother worked for. They said that they've received reports on the dig regularly, the last one arriving only a week ago. Bri accompanied her mother on the dig."

Mitsy reached up and tucked a fistful of springy red curls behind her ears, the principal's words doing nothing to calm her down. "I know. I know all of this, but something has gone wrong. Bri is the least impulsive person I've ever known. She lives every day by a strict schedule, and she's my best friend. She would not abandon me without good reason, and she wouldn't miss the wedding. She knows I'd kill her myself."

As he drummed his fingers back and forth on the top of his desk, Mitsy had to grab onto both of her elbows to keep from slamming her hand on top of his fingers. She fidgeted impatiently as she waited for him to respond.

"I'm not going to change your mind, am I? You know the days off aren't the issue. I'm just worried about you is all, as a friend, not as your principal. I don't think you are going to be happy with what you find in Scotland. I truly believe that Bri just decided to abandon her life here. It's best that you move on and forget about her. Try and enjoy the wedding and this new phase of your life."

Mitsy knew he was wrong. Every fiber of her being screamed it. She stood and made her way to the door, turning back toward him briefly. "So the days are approved? Great. I'll see you at the wedding."

Slamming the door of his office behind her, she made her way home to pack for her flight.

Chapter 4

Scotland – 1646

"Ye canna mean it, Bri? Morna's spells are unpredictable. Father told me countless stories of how her spells would go awry, causing havoc around the castle. Ye canna be sure that it will work the way ye mean it to, love."

Bri hesitated before speaking, knowing that she needed to be careful of how she approached this conversation with Eoin. She was going to do the spell regardless, she'd already made up her mind. But already in her few short months of marriage, she'd learned that if she wanted to get what she wanted, it was best to make her husband feel as if he had come up with the idea himself.

"The spell has worked correctly several times, has it not? You were even prepared to send me back with a spell. Surely you wouldn't have done so if you weren't certain that it would work correctly, right?" Bri reached out a hand to lay it on his broad shoulder, snuggling in close to weaken his resolve.

Bri smiled as Eoin buried his face in her hair, kissing the top of her head. "Aye, love. I did believe that the spell would work, but I'm so verra glad that ye dinna do it. By the time she died, Morna was a great caster."

Bri breathed in the heady scent of her husband before shaking her head to bring herself back to task. "So you see? It would be safe for me to go. You've basically just said so yourself."

A squeal escaped Bri's lips as Eoin smacked her on the behind.

"Ye are twisting me words, lass. While I do believe the spells willna cause ye harm, that doesna mean that I think ye should go. Are ye so sure that Arran feels the way ye say? I've no heard him speak of Blaire."

Stepping back so that she could look into Eoin's face, his eyes and hair a dark ebony that took her breath away, Bri smiled and continued. "Do you not remember the night of our wedding? Arran may have been drunk, but he wouldn't have kissed me so if he didn't feel there was reason to. He and Blaire had kissed before. I believe they were in love."

Bri repressed a laugh as she watched Eoin's eyebrows squish together and his lips twist in muddled confusion. "Nay! Are ye telling me that me own betrothed and me arse of a brother were together before the wedding? I should tear the lousy sot to bits."

"Oh, hush. It's not as if you loved Blaire. You couldn't stand her from what I hear, so what does it matter if Arran could? It's very hard to help who you fall in love with. Besides, if things hadn't happened as they had, it's very possible I wouldn't have ended up here. Surely you wouldn't have wanted that?"

Air quickly escaped Bri's lungs as Eoin crushed her against him, pressing his mouth to hers in a desperate kiss, leaving them both breathless as their bodies ached for more. "Nay, lass, I wouldna want that. I canna stand the thought of ye no being by me side. So, I must ask one thing of ye, if ye are to do this."

24

Her insides were weak and fluttery, hungry for more of his touch. Bri stepped away, her curiosity piqued. "What is it?"

"I shall come with ye. If the spell goes wrong, and ye are trapped in another time, I canna be away from ye."

All thoughts of lovemaking fled in an instant. "You cannot be serious, Eoin. For starters, we have no modern male clothes to put you in. I, at least, still have the clothes I was wearing when I arrived here. You would stand out like a sore thumb!"

"A sore thumb, lass?"

Confusion flickered across Eoin's face once more, and Bri couldn't help but laugh aloud. "Forget it. But that's another reason why you can't possibly come. You wouldn't be able to communicate. Not to mention how confused you will be by cars, or cell phones, ATMs." She stopped talking when Eoin reached out to place his hands on both of her shoulders.

"Aye, lass. It doesna sound so different from the way ye were when ye first arrived here. And ye survived. I shall have ye to help me, and I find meself curious to see what the world where me strange, bonny lass came from is like."

He smiled sweetly, and Bri found herself softening to the idea. It would be nice not to be all alone, and she agreed with him. If something did go wrong with the spell, she couldn't stand the thought of being separated from him. Besides, watching his reaction to the conveniences of modern times was sure to be a humorous and fascinating experience, one which now presented as a possibility, she found herself eager to take advantage of.

"Fine. But on one condition."

"Anything."

25

"While we are there, I am the boss. Life is very different and, for your own safety, you need to do whatever I tell you to do. Understood?"

Eoin rolled his eyes and Bri smiled, anticipating what he was going to say even before he spoke.

"Aye, lass. As if ye are no my master already. It shall be little adjustment from daily life now."

"That's right." Bri winked playfully. "And don't you forget it, mister. Now you'll need to think of something to tell Arran. He will have to know we are going somewhere, but it's best that he doesn't know where. He would try to stop us from going."

"Aye, he would. I shall talk to him now."

* * *

Arran made his way through the castle's winding hallways, stopping to briefly poke his head in the kitchen to pester their beloved housemaid, cook, and mentor, Mary. He stepped inside the long room and, knowing that she could see him, sneakily stuck his hand out to grab at one of the loaves of bread set aside for the evening meal.

He was rewarded with the expected quick smack on his hand.

"How many times do I have to tell ye? Ye are no going to get food from this kitchen until 'tis served to ye, as long as I am here. And doona get yer hopes up, I intend to live many more decades still."

Arran laughed and bent to scoop Mary up in a large embrace, roughly kissing her on the cheek. "Aye, I surely hope that ye do. The castle would fall apart without ye." He continued to squeeze her, her feet dangling inches off the ground, refusing to set her

26

down until she screeched and reached over his shoulder to swat at something behind him.

He quickly set the plump woman back on the floor and spun to see what had her in such arrears. Eoin stood with his hand extended in the direction of the bread, guilt spread across his face as Mary waved his brother away from the aromatic loaves.

"Ye shall drive me mad! The both of ye. It doesna matter how many times I repeat meself, ye doona seem to hear it. Now get." She paused and extended both of her arms out in front of her, palms up, and she briskly shooed them from the kitchen. "I doona want to see yer faces until the evening meal. Get on with ye."

"Aye."

"Aye."

Their voices echoed and, in unison, they each kissed Mary on the cheek and quickly made their leave of Mary's place of worship. Once outside, Arran faced Eoin.

"I've been looking for ye, brother. I need to speak with ye about the visiting clan. It's been months, and they've still made no decision. We canna allow them to stay here forever."

"Aye, ye are right. But that shall have to wait for a few days."

Arran paused as they walked together down the hallway, turning to lean against the wall so that his brother would do the same. "Has something happened?"

Eoin shook his head, and Arran instantly felt relieved. He didn't think he could bear any more tragedies so soon after the death of his father and the loss of his beloved.

"Nay, but Bran, from the village, ye remember him, aye?"

Arran nodded. "Aye, o'course. What of him?"

27

"He has asked that I come to help him with the building of a stable. He canna afford to pay anyone to help. He knew as a friend, I would. Bri shall go as well and help his wife with their brood of children."

Arran was certain Bran already had a stable, but he decided not to question his brother's story. If Eoin was gone, it would perhaps leave him with ample time to resolve the situation with their guests on his own.

"Aye, 'tis kind of ye to agree to help him. Do ye need me to go along as well?" Arran hoped Eoin would say no, but it was formality that he should offer assistance.

"Nay. I need ye to stay here and serve as laird while I'm gone. I shan't be far, but I doona want ye to try and find me with castle issues. I trust ye to see to anything that may arise while I am gone."

"O'course. Wish Bran and his family well for me. When will ye be leaving?"

"Tomorrow, I believe. I shall leave ye now. I left me wife in our bedchamber all alone. I am anxious to return to her."

Arran smiled and waved his brother off. "Aye, I'm sure ye are."

Once Eoin had left, Arran slowly made his way back to his own bedchamber. With Eoin leaving, it was the perfect opportunity for him to figure out a solution for their guests and for Edana. If he could think of a way to resolve the clan's issue of who should be laird, he knew his brother would not be upset.

If anything, he would be pleased to have things around the castle calm down to their normal pace. And he knew it would do himself good to have something else to focus his mind upon. He might not love Edana, but he could make sure that she was taken care of. Aye, as far as he was concerned, his brother's trip to the village could not have come at a better time.

Chapter 5

Edinburgh, Scotland – Present Day

I was certain I'd never heard such language from a lady. I did my best to listen to the angry woman, but with each breath her voice grew louder, and I found my mind drifting away from the conversation. Not that I was given much chance to speak. The old lady waved her finger at me in such a manner, I was certain it would fall off.

A momentary second of silence caused me to refocus my attention.

"'Ello? Are ye daft in the head? Have ye been listening to a word I've said to ye?" Danny threw her hands violently up in the air only to bring them down swiftly so they sat snugly on her hips. My boss glared at me, unblinking, until I opened my mouth to speak.

"Aye. I did hear ye, but I doona understand. There's no reason why the two of them should have been asleep so late in the day. They werena sick, and 'tis dreadful behavior." I knew my words were to be met with more screaming and, unconsciously, I felt the tips of my ears pull back as they readied themselves for the inevitable attack.

"Ye are a bloody fool! If only I had the luxury of sleeping in one day in me lousy life, I would take full advantage. It is not yer place to decide how long our paying guests sleep in the morning.

I've told ye before, if they are in the room, skip it and go on to the next room for cleaning. Come back to it later, after they awake and leave for the day."

"Aye, I willna do it again." I turned to leave, hoping that if I slipped away fast enough, the lecture would be over. I only stepped one step away before Danny reached to grab me by my arm.

"Ye turn back around. I dinna dismiss ye. Ye are right, ye willna do it again because ye are no longer employed by the hotel."

Danny looked at me, satisfaction evident on her face, but as I continued to adjust to the many unfamiliar words of this time, I dinna understand what she was telling me. "I'm sorry. I doona understand ye. No longer employed?"

"Fired. Doona show up for work here again. I doona want to see ye around here. If this was yer first transgression, then ye would only be getting a warning, but there have been many complaints."

Twas cold, but sweat beaded on me forehead, understanding settling in. I no longer had a job. "Complaints?"

"Aye, lass. Complaints. Many. More than one family said they saw ye sweeping the carpet rather than using the vacuum. Another said they saw ye hanging the sheets up in the room to be beaten with the broom handle. Who taught ye to clean? Yer great-great-great grandmother?" Danny laughed slightly, pleased with herself for the odd joke.

"No one taught me to clean. I doona like the sound of the vacuum, it hurts me ears. And I doona know how to use the cleaning barrel for the sheets."

Danny's eyes grew wide at my ignorance.

"Cleaning barrel? Do ye mean the washing machine? Gracious! I'd hate to see what yer house looks like, and I bet yer

31

clothes smell something dreadful. Now, collect yer things and be gone with ye."

She gave me no further chance to speak as she turned and left, leaving me alone in the small storage room beneath the staircase. I knew I'd been in trouble when she pulled me into the broom storage, but I never expected to be left without a job.

Without it, I had little means to pay for the small apartment Jerry and Morna found for me, and I was unsure of how to search for another job. What could I do? I had few skills, and those I did possess would serve me little in today's time.

I'd held the job for only two weeks and, with each passing day, I found myself regretting me decision to stay in this time just a little bit more.

But it dinna matter. I alone had chosen my path. Breathing in deeply as I tried to suck back the tears threatening to fall from the corner of my eye, I lifted my head up as I left the closet.

* * *

"Wait up!"

I heard the shout from behind my shoulder but continued to make my way home, assuming the words were meant for someone else.

"Blaire! Slow down. Ye walk so fast I canna catch up to ye."

I stopped walking, causing a man who seemed to be in quite a big hurry to walk right into my back. After he told me what he thought about me in a few short, fairly shocking words, I turned to see one of the other maids, Isla, lifting her dainty, short legs up in an effort to reach me.

"I'm sorry. I thought ye were calling after someone else."

Once she was next to me, we moved off of the main walkway so that we could stand without blocking the way of others. Isla rubbed her gloved hands together and cupped them around her mouth, blowing air into them to warm her hands.

I continued to be amazed at how cold everyone seemed to always be. Twas no colder than Scotland always was and, with the thick coats and protective clothing that people now wore, not to mention my favorite modern invention—heaters—I found the temperature to always be quite enjoyable.

"No, I was talking to ye. I just got off work, and I heard about what Danny did to ye. I'm sorry that ye lost yer job, but I do have to tell ye, ye did do things awful strange. But that's not what I wanted to tell ye. I might could get ye another job if ye like."

"Aye, I would like. I doona know what I will do for a job."

Isla smiled and put her arm around me as if we were more closely acquainted than we actually were. "I thought that might be the case. There is a catch, though. Ye canna do this job looking like ye do. It would only cause trouble for ye."

I stepped away, still uncomfortable with the familiarity that people of this time used with one another. "What do ye mean? What is the job?"

"Me cousin owns a pub not far from the hotel. I've been bartending there as a second job, but I canna juggle both at the same time. He's looking for a replacement for me. I would train ye meself, and I know he will give ye the job if I ask him. All ye do is mix drinks, but ye look too pretty and sweet with yer long hair and clean face. I know ye have enough spunk to handle the job, but yer appearance needs to reflect yer no-nonsense attitude. I'll help ye change yer look. What do ye say?" Isla smiled and shrugged her shoulders, raising her hands palm up as if awaiting my answer.

33

I knew it would be foolish to tell her no. "Aye, I canna thank ye enough, Isla. What do ye want to do about the way I look?"

I fidgeted uncomfortably while Isla looked me up and down, deciding how to best alter what appeared to be so unacceptable. "How would ye feel about cutting yer hair? And maybe piercing yer ears? And eyeliner, ye definitely need to learn how to implore the use of eyeliner. It will make ye look more intimidating instantly, and believe me, when tending bar for a bunch of rowdy Scots, ye want a look that says 'doona even think about it'."

"Aye, if ye say so. But I doona wanna look like a man. The hair goes no higher than me shoulders." I reached a hand up to run through my long locks. Mayhap a change would be good.

"Deal."

With that, Isla led me in another direction, away from my new home. We walked for what seemed liked miles, my feet heavy and tired from working all day at the hotel. Several blocks past the street leading to where we'd both previously worked, Isla turned us onto a dimly lit street where we made our way into what she called a hair "salon."

I was seated quickly. As the woman behind me snipped away at my long, dark hair, I kept my eyes focused upon the floor. I dinna want to see my reflection in the mirror, each snap of her scissors causing my heart to beat a little faster.

After cutting what I was sure was every hair off the top of my head, she took out a large and frightening object that shot out warm air that she blew onto my wet strands. Once all of them were dry, she continued to mess and spray odd potions into my hair as I sat nervously in the seat. By the time she finished, the city was engulfed in darkness, small street lamps the only visible light outside the window.

34

"Are ye ready?" They were the first words the woman had spoken to me. With my mouth dry I simply nodded, keeping my eyes squeezed shut as she turned me to face the mirror. "Open yer eyes, dear. If ye doona like it, it's only hair. It'll grow back."

Her argument was sound and slowly I opened my eyes, unable to stop the wide smile that spread across my features as I took in my glorious reflection.

While I was certain I was going to find myself without hair, she'd actually kept a good amount. With the ends lightly curled around my shoulders, each strand of hair seemed to find new life, no longer weighted down.

"I love it." I smiled and stood, hesitantly reaching a hand out to pat the woman on the shoulder. Twas a gesture that seemed acceptable in this time, and now that my hair seemed to fit, I thought I could at least make an effort to make my behaviors fit as well.

"Great. Now, on to make up and piercing." Isla stood, extending money toward the hairdresser before motioning that I follow her out of the shop.

The next place we found one block further down and located on a street even more dimly lit than the last. Situated in between two stores on either side, which claimed to draw pictures on people's skin, we made our way inside the frightening looking shop.

Once again, I was thrust into a seat and handled as the man working obeyed Isla's orders and held different shapes and sizes of objects up to my ear. Once Isla found one that satisfied her, I was told to sit back and not move as there would soon be a prick.

I relaxed, certain that a prick would be no worse than being stuck by a pin whilst being fitted for a dress. As the man squeezed his fingers together over a foreign contraption, and I felt the rod of the object pierce my skin, I let out a howl I was sure the Conalls could hear all the way back in 1646.

Chapter 6

Conall Castle – 1646

"Are ye sure that ye wanna go through with it? I willna be able to sleep a wink while ye are both away. I think ye are being foolish, but ye never wish to listen to me." Mary fluttered nervously around the spell room, rambling as she listed reasons why Eoin and Bri should not try and go forward to retrieve Blaire, only stopping when she was interrupted by Adelle, who stood anxiously in the doorway.

"She's right. I miss Blaire, but I'd rather the two of you didn't risk your own lives to go look for her."

The two women continued to rant back and forth, talking more to each other than to Eoin or Bri, each doing their best to proclaim themselves as alpha among the mother and mother-figure duo.

Bri looked over her shoulder at Eoin, who had his arms wrapped around her to hold her close. "They aren't going to stop until we are gone, you know that, right? It's best that we get going. It will take us a few hours to walk to the inn, and we are going to have some explaining to do about your clothing if we run into anyone at the castle or along the road."

"Aye lass, I suppose ye are right. What are we to tell them again?"

Eoin squeezed Bri tightly, and she sighed in response to the comfort of his warm arms around her before responding. "Well, let's hope that we don't bump into anyone who works at the castle, like a tour guide. If we do, we will just tell them that you wanted to dress up to get into the spirit of things. They will think you're crazy, but any girl that sees you is just going to be so pleased they had the opportunity to gaze upon you shirtless, I doubt they will care much about your sanity."

Bri smiled as he chuckled deeply into her ear. "I doona think that is so, lass. I'm no so uncommon looking."

"Pfff...yeah, whatever." She paused to twist and give him a swift kiss on the lips. "Let's shut these two yappers up and get out of here. You ready?"

"Aye. Do ye wanna get their attention or should I?"

"I'll do it. I know just how to get a response out of Mom." Bri smiled before she shouted, "Adelle!" in her mother's direction. Instantly, her mother's eyes widened and whipped toward her, awarding Bri with a stern expression.

"What? I know that you didn't just call me 'Adelle,' right? I'm your mother."

Bri stepped away from Eoin and looked up at him. "Told ya," she whispered before moving to pull her mother into a hug. "We're leaving now, Mom. It's going to be fine. Morna's spells seem to be pretty reliable." Bri pulled away from her mother's vice-like embrace and moved over to hug Mary. "Now, both of you try not to worry while we're gone. It may be a few weeks before we get back. Just keep yourselves busy."

It was Mary's turn to react. "Do ye no think that I always keep meself busy? Do ye think that I just lie around the castle, trying to dream up things to do?"

Bri rolled her eyes and stepped back so that Eoin could bid both of the women farewell. "No, of course I don't think that,

Mary, and you know it. Now remember, don't let Arran find out where we've gone off to. He'll find out soon enough if Blaire wants to return. If she doesn't, I don't want him getting his hopes up."

Both women nodded and, when it was clear that Bri and Eoin were about to begin the spell, they quietly retreated from the small room.

Standing in front of the old, faded book, Bri took Eoin's hands. Together they lit the candles and read aloud the words from the book. Momentary shockwaves of pain coursed through them. They wrapped their arms around one another, and together, vanished from the room.

* * *

Muffled voices became audible above their heads. Both groggy and confused, they leaned against the walls of the once familiar room until they found themselves reoriented. Having already made the trip through once, Bri knew instantly the headache Eoin would have and went straight for her mother's backpack, still tucked neatly behind the bench in front of the table, out of sight from the eyes of wandering tourists.

Opening the inner zipper pocket, she pulled out the bottle of Advil and dumped out five round pills into her hand, two for herself and three for her beast of a husband. They had no water, but if either of them were to function, they had to medicate the head trauma that always seemed to occur when travelling through time by Morna's spells.

"Here." Shakily, she moved to stand in front of Eoin, her legs still slightly unsteady and discombobulated. "Put these in your mouth and swallow them. They will help with your headache."

Obligingly, Eoin held open his hand as he looked down at the pills questioningly. "What are they, lass? They look too small to do much for me head."

Bri slowly raised his hand to motion for him to put them in his mouth. "Trust me. They'll help. But at least it looks like we made it. Look at how old everything in the room looks."

Bri smiled as she watched Eoin wander about the room awestruck. She reached a hand in his direction as she moved to the door leading to the staircase out of the basement. "Did you hear the voices above us just a moment ago? I think they must be conducting a tour. No surprise really, since we were able to stop the castle from being destroyed. I'm sure it's quite the tourist attraction today. Which means it's going to be difficult for us to get out of the castle unseen."

Eoin winked, and Bri smiled at the playfulness in his eyes. "Aye. I expect since I have ye with me, it shall be impossible. Ye are talented at falling down. I'm certain I will have to scoop ye off the floor at least twice before we make our escape."

Bri whispered as she leaned her ear against the spell room door, listening for any sign of movement on the other side. "What about you? You're not so light on your feet yourself. Now, let's go. I don't hear anybody on the other side."

Cautiously, Bri pulled the door open, finding the main basement room empty. As she closed the secret door to the spell room behind them, she could tell that it had remained unfound despite the years of tourism at the castle. The only sign of entrance within the basement was an "employees only" sign that was draped across the floor in front of the staircase leading up out of the basement.

Hesitantly, Bri climbed the stairs and gently pulled at the door. The ridged nature of the door's hinges showed her that not even castle employees went down into the basement very often.

But as luck would have it, just as Eoin had securely shut the spell room door, hiding it away from view, they both heard the door at the top of the basement stairs open. Listening to the sound of footsteps descend the staircase, they soon found themselves staring back at the very official-looking castle employee whose eyes widened in shock at the sight of them.

* * *

Scotland – Present Day

Mitsy soon-to-be Fredrickson angrily slammed the door and stood to straighten out her shirt and pull up her pants before making her way to the front door of the small roadside inn. Her connecting flight out of Chicago had been delayed a whopping six hours, cutting the time that she could spend searching for Bri in Scotland short by almost an entire day.

Not to mention the time it had taken her to rent a car and find a decent map, none of which seemed to show the location of the inn. Hours later, frustrated, tired, and worried as hell, Mitsy found herself standing in front of the last place Bri had supposedly been seen.

She hoped Bri was safe, but part of her knew that if she walked into that inn to find Bri lounging around as if on vacation, she was going to kill her AWOL maid of honor on the spot.

41

Determined to find an answer, she rapped her knuckles against the wooden door, knocking with as much authority as she could muster.

The door swung open quickly and, with her hands still rapidly moving in a knocking motion, she nearly knocked on the old man's head who now stood before her, smiling. "Come in, lass. Why do ye seem to be in such a hurry? We've plenty of rooms if ye are looking for a place to stay."

Mitsy stepped inside, her angry resolve slipping slightly at the friendliness in the man's eyes. Surely he couldn't be responsible for anything that happened to Bri. Stopping just inside the doorway, she spoke, "I'm not looking for a room. I'm looking for a person that was supposedly staying here. Brielle Montgomery. She's been missing for some time now, and the police have closed the investigation because they spoke to you and your wife, and you told them that she was fine. She can't be fine. She wouldn't just leave without giving me an explanation. Where is she?"

Mitsy watched as the man's brows creased together, as if he was unsure of how to answer, and she immediately grew suspicious.

"Why doona ye follow me into the kitchen, lass, and we can talk about yer friend?"

Mitsy lightly stomped her foot against the ground in an effort to root herself firmly in place. "I don't think so, sir. I think you need to tell me whatever it is you know about Bri right this instant."

"Gwendolyn, can ye come in here, sweetheart? We have a visitor who is looking for Bri." The man paused and, while waiting for his wife to arrive, extended a hand in Mitsy's direction and said, "My name is Jerry. And ye might be?"

Mitsy didn't accept his hand, only curtly giving her name before his wife rounded the corner from the kitchen and came to stand in front of her. "I'm Mitsy. Now, your wife is here. Tell me where Bri is."

Mitsy watched hesitantly as Gwendolyn approached her, smiling.

"I'm afraid she's not here. She moved to Edinburgh only a few weeks ago. She's working as a maid in a hotel, I believe. If ye like, I can give ye directions to the place."

Shock coursed through her as she took in the old woman's words. Hotel maid? Moved? Why would Bri suddenly decide to drastically change her life? It didn't make sense. Her voice was shaky when she tried to speak. "Y-Yes. Please. I would appreciate directions."

Holding the small pad in which Gwendolyn had written direction to where Bri was supposedly located, Mitsy turned and made her way back to the car. She didn't care that she was so tired she could hardly keep her eyes open and so hungry that the sheep in the fields looked appetizing, she was going to find Bri tonight.

* * *

"Why did ye tell the lass that Bri was in Edinburgh? Doona ye remember that it is Blaire living there?" Jerry looked at his wife with concern only to be rewarded with a soft smack on his arm.

"O'course I know 'tis Blaire. Doona ye worry about it, dear. The real Bri is on her way to us as we speak. Once she gets here, we will send her in the same direction as Mitsy."

43

Chapter 7

I glanced out of the corner of my eye, watching Mik as he gathered his coat and made his way to the door. Nearing half past ten, we were supposed to remain open until midnight. I had every intention of closing down the pub as soon as Mik left.

He paused at the door and turned to me. "Are ye sure that ye doona mind closing alone, Blaire? I know that it was yer turn to leave early, only some of me friends are throwing a party and..."

I held a hand up to stop him. "Aye, 'tis fine. I doona mind."

He smiled and opened the front door, sending a blast of frigid air through the room. He paused before walking out and turned his head back in me direction.

"Ye are welcome to stop by after if ye'd like."

He dinna wait for my response and, as the door shut, I reached behind me for a wet rag, hurriedly wiping down the counters. If the owner found out, I'd be sure to take the blame. I dinna want Mik to get in trouble for me decision to close, but it was Thursday evening and the pub's only customer was the ancient drunkard who had spent every night here since my first evening tending bar.

Once the counter was wiped clean, I circled the tables gathering glasses to put in the dishwasher. Every time I started the strange machine, I couldna help but smile. 'Twas a miraculous invention and much more pleasant than the vacuum and other cleaning instruments of this time. 'Twas much more quiet, and the swishing of the water was a sound I found soothing.

Giving the room another glance to ensure that everything was clean and ready for those working the next day's opening shift, I made my way to the telephone hanging on the side wall. Pulling out the number Isla had given me, I dialed the number to call for a taxi. Telephones were a convenience that were quite useful on evenings like this when I had no one to help me make sure the old man found his way home. But other than a few occasions, the ease at which people could contact one another in this time made me uneasy.

It seemed to me that people in the twenty-first century became anxious too quickly after not hearing from someone because they have grown so accustomed to remaining in constant contact. 'Tis much easier to wait for news if ye know 'tis going to be a long time before ye hear any than 'tis to constantly be aware that every second could bring change.

Pushing my musings aside, I walked over to the old man who was now slumped over and snoring. I did my best to rouse him from his slumber as I waited for the taxi that would take the man home.

* * *

"What do you mean she doesn't work here? I was just told that she did." Well past twenty-four hours without sleep, Mitsy's exhaustion started to idle her brain. With each word that she spoke, she grew more frustrated and had to blink back tears to keep herself from throwing a temper tantrum in the middle of the small hotel lobby. Waiting for the response, she glared back at the nervous looking girl behind the front desk.

"I do apologize, miss. I only started last week, and I've never heard of anyone who works here with the name Bri. It's possible that she does, and we've never worked the same shift. Give me just a moment and I'll go and ask a few of the maids."

"Yes. Please." Mitsy spotted a lounge chair in the corner and collapsed onto the worn seat. She reached up, placing her fingertips on her eyelids as she pried them open, staring blankly at the carpet in an effort to stay awake. A hand on her shoulder caused her to jump, poking herself in the eye. "Damnit!" She stood, flailing exaggeratedly as she straightened and pulled at the bottom of her shirt before looking up at the person in front of her.

"Sorry, miss. This is Isla. She says that she knows the person ye are looking for, but I was right, she no longer works here, and her name isna Bri." The front desk clerk stepped back allowing Isla to come into Mitsy's view.

"Hello. I'm Isla. Is it perhaps Blaire that ye are looking for, miss? Dark hair, blue eyes, terrible maid. I doona know a Bri who has worked here."

Mitsy swallowed the lump in her throat and pushed her hair behind her ears as she repressed the frustration building once again. "No. I'm not looking for someone named Blaire. I'm looking for a Brielle Montgomery. Everybody calls her Bri. She's American. She does have dark hair and blue eyes, but I'd be very surprised if she was a terrible maid. That woman is the most anal, organized, nasty-nice person I know. Now I just spoke with an elderly couple who told me that they'd helped secure her a job here. It's very important that I find her."

"Hmm. I doona know a Bri, miss. The only person that I can think of is Blaire. She wasna American, but her accent was a little odd, and she never told any of us where she came from or why she was here. Do ye think that she could have been putting it on? Is she running from something?"

Mitsy stepped back and sat down into the chair once again as the woman's words sunk in. She didn't think that Bri would go to the effort of changing her name and using an accent, but then again, she never would have thought she'd be traipsing all over Scotland looking for her either. She stood and gathered her things. "I don't know. Can you tell me where this Blaire is now? My only option is to at least see if she's Bri."

"Sure. She's working at my cousin's pub. It's no far from here. I can point ye in the direction. I doona know if she's working now, but ye can at least go and see."

After being shown the way by Isla, Mitsy uttered a thank you and took off as quickly as her sleep-deprived body would carry her.

* * *

The taxi arrived in just under half an hour, and the old man still sat slumped over a small table at the back of the room. After agreeing to pay the taxi driver double what it would cost to get the man home, he agreed to come inside and help me get the drunk into the car.

Twenty minutes later, I gathered up my empty wallet, put on my coat, and flipped the lights off as I made my way to the front doors to lock up for the night. I fumbled to get a grip on the correct key with my bulky gloves. Finally giving up, I bit the end of one of

47

my gloves allowing me to slip it off so that I could get a better grasp on the slippery keys.

The street around me was dark, and I hurried as best I could, not wanting to linger any longer than necessary. I twisted and pulled on the handle to ensure it locked and was just slipping my glove back on when a loud voice to the left caused me to drop the glove and keys.

"Oh my God, Bri! It is you. I am going to freaking kill you! Open that door back up, right now, because we are about to have quite the conversation, and I'd rather not freeze to death while doing so."

I dinna move to pick up my belongings and stared back at the strange, red-haired woman. The only word I'd been able to understand from her was Bri, and I wasna sure of how to deal with the woman's sudden appearance. Obviously, she was someone who had known Adelle's daughter and, from her manner of speaking, I could only assume she'd known her quite well.

"Oh. Surprised to see me, are you? What? Did you really think you could just skip out on your entire life and not expect anyone to come looking for you? You weren't that much of a loner, Bri. There are people who care about you. I care about you! Now, quit staring at me like I'm the one who's lost my mind. Open that damn door, or I will open it myself."

In an effort to allow myself a few moments to think on my best course of action, I bent to retrieve my glove and the keys to the pub and obeyed the woman's orders by opening the door. Assuming she would follow, I made my way inside and flipped on the lights. I knew I couldna pretend to be Bri. If she knew her well, it would be impossible. "May I ask yer name? I'm no Bri. My name is Blaire." I paused, guilt at the woman's pain causing me to shift nervously. The woman's eyes bulged, and her face reddened.

"You have got to be joking me. You do realize that coming to find you has cost me several months' salary, and that's something I really can't afford considering I've been busy planning a wedding for the last year and a half? Or did you forget about that, too?"

I squished up my nose, knowing whatever I said was going to upset her. "I'm verra sorry, miss, but I truly doona know who ye are."

"Sorry! Well then. I'm sorry for this as well, but I bet that when I'm finished, you'll remember who I am and who you are just fine."

I wasn't sure what the women meant, but as she lunged toward me, I knew she meant to cause me some sort of physical pain, and I moved quickly out of her path beginning our odd dance of lunge and dash around the empty room.

Chapter 8

Present Day – Conall Castle

Bri glanced uncomfortably at her half-dressed husband before turning back to face the shocked custodian. "Hello," Bri smiled as sweetly as she could and reached behind her until she found Eoin's hand, pulling him up the stairs behind her as she continued out of the stairwell. "We were just leaving."

Looking down, Bri did her best to scoot by the man, hoping they would be able to exit without further explanation. Her mother had told her once that if you walked with authority and pretended like you were somewhere you were supposed to be, people were less likely to question your behavior. It had worked well for her mother, allowing Adelle to ransack through more museum displays than Bri could count. She sensed she would not have the same success rate and knew she was right as the man moved to stand in front of her, blocking their exit from the basement.

"Now, I know that ye both must have seen the 'Do Not Enter' sign on the front of this door. What made ye think that the sign dinna apply to the two of ye?"

Eoin started to speak, and Bri quickly threw an elbow into his ribs to silence him. The feeling of his bare chest against her skin gave her an idea. Before allowing herself to think it through, she threw her right arm over Eoin's shoulder and snuggled in close to reach over and kiss his cheek. "I'm sorry, sir. You see, we are visiting the area on our honeymoon, and the castle is just so romantic. We are having a hard enough time keeping our hands off each other as it is. When our tour group walked by here, I just decided to take the opportunity to slip away for a few moments with my new husband." Not waiting for the man to respond, Bri turned and pressed herself up against Eoin, kissing him hard on the mouth.

She allowed the kiss to go on for a few moments, intent on making her point to the castle employee. Finally, hearing the man clear his throat uncomfortably, Bri pulled away from an open-mouthed, grinning Eoin to hear the custodian's response.

"Ah, well there are certain places for such things, and this isna one of them. I should have ye escorted out immediately, but seeing as ye are newlyweds, I'll cut the two of ye a break, aye? But I doona want to catch ye somewhere that ye shouldn't be again. And why the hell are ye no wearing a shirt, man?"

Bri watched as the man shifted his attention to Eoin, and once again, Bri nudged an elbow of warning into her husband's ribs. She waved a hand flippantly in the air. "Oh. That. It's a costume. He wanted to, ya know, get into the spirit of things."

The man didn't respond, only moved out of their way so that they could exit the stairwell. Shutting the door behind them, Bri started to thank him but stopped as the man chuckled once, muttering "Americans" under his breath before shaking his head and turning to leave them alone in the empty hallway.

"Lass, I know I agreed that ye would be in charge during our journey here, but do ye really think that was the best way to handle it? That man thinks that we are both mad, and the way ye dinna allow me to speak, why he must think I'm a mute."

51

Bri laughed, slightly shocked at her own behavior. "I'm sorry. I didn't know what to do. When I felt your bare chest behind me, it was the only thing that popped in my head. But what does it matter anyway? It worked, didn't it? Now, let's get out of here before another tour passes by. I don't want to have to explain your clothing again." Dragging her husband along behind her, they made their way out of the castle without seeing another soul.

* * *

"Do ye think that she will still be here? If she wanted a different life for herself, this hardly seems the place."

Bri knocked on the door of the inn before answering Eoin's question. "No, I doubt that she is, but perhaps they will know where to find her. But it might be a bit of a tricky situation. They thought that Blaire was me, so I'm not sure how we are going to explain my sudden appearance, not to mention yours."

The door opened, startling both of them. Before Bri could utter a hello, she was pulled into Jerry's rail-thin arms.

"Bri, it's good to see ye again, lass. And Eoin, ye sure are quite the big lad, are ye no? Me wife will be quite pleased to see ye. Now come inside." Jerry waved them into the living room and shouted in the direction of the kitchen. "They're here, dear."

Bri was certain her mouth hung open as she glanced back at Eoin whose pinched brows and wide eyes matched her own. Once seated, Jerry excused himself, and Bri leaned over to whisper to Eoin, "Did he just call you by your name? How could he possibly know that?"

Eoin answered absent-mindedly as he glanced around the room. "I doona know. Bri, how is the room lit? I doona think the flames above our heads would be easily lit or put out."

Bri smiled and pointed to the light switch on the wall. "They aren't flames. It's electricity. All you have to do to turn them on is flip that tiny switch over there. Flipping it in the other direction will turn the lights off."

"Ye canna mean it? What a change from our dark, candle lit rooms. Tell me, will we be alive to see lights such as this?"

"No, I'm afraid not. You'll see lots of amazing things while we are here, and I can't wait to watch you discover them, but first..." Bri paused as Jerry re-entered the room, Gwendolyn trailing him. Bri stood to give the old woman a hug and, once she returned to her seat back on the couch, Gwendolyn spoke up.

"Bri, you don't need to worry about how you are going to explain your situation to us. We know that while you were here with your mother at the beginning, it was Blaire for most of the time. In fact, I believe I have some things I must explain to both of you. But first, I'd like to kiss my nephew."

She moved across the room, grabbing Eoin by both cheeks as she brought him near to her and kissed him on the forehead.

Bri's mind reeled at the spectacle when Jerry's voice to her right drew her attention.

"Ach, lassie. That's no even half of it. Ye best settle in and prepare yerself for some interesting news."

* * *

Nearing eleven, Bri and Eoin pulled up in the car they'd borrowed from Jerry as Bri parked it in front of the pub where

Blaire supposedly now worked. The lights were on inside, and while she couldn't see Blaire through the windows, she hoped that their search for her would end, and their evening of overwhelming surprises would be over.

"Are you ready? Blaire already knows you, so I think it might be best if you speak to her first." Bri reached for the door handle but paused at the touch of Eoin's hand on her forearm.

"Did ye believe her story, Bri? Do ye think 'tis possible that she really is my Aunt Morna?"

"Yes, I do. After all that we've been through, I find it very difficult to be surprised anymore. Are you all right? Does it upset you to know that she's been here?"

Bri rubbed Eoin's arm to comfort him as he shook his head. "No. I only wish me father was here to see her. He missed her dearly after she was gone. He'd be so pleased to know that she is loved and happy. He was the only one around her that dinna fear her witchcraft."

"Well, it seems your father was right. I don't think there is any reason to fear Morna. I for one will be forever grateful for all she has done. I wouldn't have you otherwise." Bri leaned in briefly to lightly kiss Eoin on the cheek. "Now, let's get in there and see to Blaire."

"Aye, I doona like 'cars.' Nothing should be able to move so quickly. 'Tisna natural."

Bri laughed as they exited the car and walked to the door of the pub. "You go first. I'm nervous to see my look-a-like." She gently nudged Eoin's back, urging him to try the lock.

"Aye, fine. But I doona believe ye should be nervous. I should, however. I doona expect the lass will be too pleased to see me."

The door was unlocked, and they stepped inside to the chaotic scene of overturned chairs and tables with Blaire lying in the corner straddled by some woman whose face they could not see as the two women screamed incoherently at one another.

"Eoin! Go get that woman off of her. What is she doing?"

Bri approached cautiously, standing back to watch as Eoin dragged the two women apart, pulling the redhead away from Blaire.

Blaire stood quickly and looked down at herself to brush off the bottom of her pants, and Bri knew that she'd yet to see her or to recognize the man holding her assailant. "Thank ye. The woman is mad."

The woman in question screamed in protest and threw her head back sending the red curls that covered her face backward, revealing her face.

Bri gasped aloud in recognition as she rushed toward her old friend. "Mitsy?"

"Bri?" Mitsy lunged in an effort to escape Eoin's arms as Blaire looked up for the first time.

"Eoin?"

As shock and recognition flickered among the strange foursome, more chaos ensued.

Chapter 9

I looked up to see, by far, the most surprising thing since I'd arrived in this century. Not only was my ex-fiancé staring back at me, but so was the woman who looked so much like myself that I knew she must be Bri.

When I decided to stay here, I'd been certain I would never see anyone I'd previously known ever again, but to witness Eoin standing before me meant that obviously Morna's spells were not as close-ended as we originally thought.

After I recognized Eoin and shouted his name in question, my attacker noticed the woman standing next to me. More screaming followed as shock reverberated through everyone in the room, save Eoin. He eventually quieted us all by slamming his fist down so roughly against the table that it seemed to shake the room.

"Quiet, all three of ye! 'Tis been a long day, and I doona think I can take such noise any longer."

Recognizing the seriousness in his tone, the three of us quieted instantly, but only a moment passed before the redheaded mad woman spoke again.

"Somebody better tell me just what the hell is going on here, or I'm about to lose it on every single one of you." The redhead paused and pointed a shaky finger in Bri's direction. "Now, you are Bri, right? If you tell me you're not, I swear I will jump on top of you as well. How did I not know you had a twin?"

I leaned back against the wall behind me, confused as to Eoin and Bri's arrival here as well, but quite entertained with the exchange taking place between the two women.

"She's not my twin. I'm not related to her at all as far as I know. Mitsy, what are you doing here?" Bri asked.

Anger flashed in the redhead's face who now had the name of Mitsy and, for a moment, I was certain she was going to try and leap out of Eoin's restraining arms once more.

"What am I doing here? You have got to be kidding me! What are you doing here? God, Bri, I thought you were dead! You've been gone for months with no word or explanation. Your trip to Scotland with your mother was only supposed to last a few weeks. I've been trying to locate you ever since the police stopped their investigation. You're supposed to be in my wedding, Bri! I can't believe you just left everything. Were you really just not going to show?" Mitsy relaxed in Eoin's hold as she collapsed into a fit of sobs. She seemed genuinely distraught. As Bri moved in to comfort her friend, Eoin released his grip as Bri gathered Mitsy into her arms. "I'm so angry at you! I want to kill you myself." Mitsy choked on her tears.

Bri ushered her away from Eoin and myself.

"I know. Let's move over here and talk so that I can explain what's happened to you. It will give Eoin and Blaire a chance to get reacquainted."

As the two women moved toward the bar, I dinna miss the apologetic look Bri shot in Eoin's direction, presumably for leaving him alone with me. Without doubt, my relationship with Eoin had always been slightly contentious but only because I dinna want to marry him. If I'd known him under any under circumstance, I suspected we would've gotten along just fine. I found myself a little embarrassed to know that Bri had heard of my terrible behavior toward him.

"Eoin." I nodded once and stood quietly, determined to let him initiate conversation. Always the gentlemen, he moved to pick up my hand and kiss it lightly before stepping away once more.

"Blaire, ye look well. Do ye enjoy being here in this time, lass? It's verra different from our own. Are ye happy?"

His question surprised me, and I couldna help but wonder if perhaps I wasna doing as good a job at looking happy as I was trying to do. Truth was, I was lonely. And while I loved the independence women enjoyed in this time, I missed my home. But I knew it was most likely impossible for me to return and, even if I could, I dinna think I could stand the heartache that would come with being near Arran and knowing I was unwanted.

It took me a moment too long to answer Eoin, and I knew he could read the untruth behind my words. "Aye. O'course I'm happy. Why wouldna I be? Why are ye here, Eoin? I'm verra surprised to see ye."

Eoin chuckled. "Aye, I suppose that ye are. I'm surprised to find meself here as well. Bri wished to come to take care of some things that were left unfinished from her life here. I wouldna let her go alone. If something happened, I doona think I could go back to a life without her."

"I'm glad that ye are happy, Eoin. Is all well with yer family? Have ye heard from me father?" I dinna mention Arran, but something in Eoin's eyes made me wonder if he knew it was Arran I was asking about. Was it possible that Eoin knew about what had occurred between his brother and me? If so, perhaps Arran had not closed his heart so completely to me. The thought gave way for a small trickle of hope to rise within me, one which I quickly pushed away while I waited for Eoin's response.

He waved me to a table in the corner of the room. "It looks as if they may be a while. Let us sit, and I'll tell ye all that has happened while ye have been away."

I nodded and followed, glancing quickly at the two women visiting at the bar. As I watched them, I remembered the shocked expression on Bri's face when she realized the woman Eoin was holding back was Mitsy. Bri hadn't known her friend would be here. Eoin had lied. They had not come to the pub so that Bri could give Mitsy an explanation, they'd come here looking for me.

* * *

"Did you tell her why we came here?" Bri led the way to their hotel room as Eoin slowly made his way down the hallway, stopping every so often to stare at something new that fascinated him. Several hours after arriving at the pub, they'd all left together, first dropping Blaire off at her apartment and next securing two hotel rooms for the three of them just across the street from Blaire's place of residence. With Mitsy shut away in her room for the evening, Bri and Eoin were finally able to discuss what had occurred over the last few hours.

"I dinna tell her all of why we came here. I told her that ye needed to see to some things ye'd left unfinished, but I dinna tell her that we'd come to see if she would return home."

Bri stopped in front of their room and pulled the plastic key card from her pocket. Smiling, she extended it Eoin's direction. "Here. You see that slot above the handle? Stick this card in there and then slowly pull it out. It will unlock the door."

It took him three tries but Bri remained patient, enjoying the look of awe that radiated from her husband's face. Once inside, she decided to tell him the news she'd dreaded sharing with him since they'd left the pub.

"Well, I suppose it's fine that you haven't told her the other reason we came here, just yet. You'll have plenty of time to do that."

She heard her husband stop playing with the toilet in the bathroom, and she knew she'd caught his attention. "What do ye mean by that, lass? Now that ye have spoken with yer friend, we should be able to return home in only a few days, aye?"

Bri shook her head and turned a guilty face on her husband. "No. I'm afraid not. You and Blaire are going to have the next week all to yourselves. I made a promise over a year ago that I would be Mitsy's maid of honor. I'm leaving with her tomorrow to go back to the States for her wedding."

Chapter 10

Conall Castle - 1646

Tormod Kinnaird left the clan gathering more determined than ever to find a way to take over as laird. In his mind, it was his by right anyway. He was the eldest son of Ramsay Kinnaird's younger brother, but a bastard son, and therefore unrecognized by all but his mother and sister as a true Kinnaird.

The same meeting had been held every night since the death of his uncle, and everyone grew restless as little progress had been made in determining the best way to declare a new laird. Many members of the clan wished to return home and wait to declare a new leader until a way was agreed upon, but the majority of people knew this would leave them without a clear leader for protection and would make them look weak in the eyes of neighboring clans—a sure way to invite further conflict and violence.

The only decision that they'd all agreed upon was that Edana would not be placed out of her home, which left him to assume that whomever became laird would marry Edana. Only a few men remained unmarried within the clan and, although he didn't know for sure if Edana would be given any choice in who she married, he intended to make sure her first choice would be him.

Though improper for him to be in the castle's main bedchamber hallway at this time of evening, with Eoin Conall away and his drunk of a brother left to manage things, Tormod was almost certain he would be able to sneak into Edana's room unnoticed.

He had seen Edana enter the room at the end of the hallway enough times during their stay here to know that was where she roomed. He stood in front of the door unsure whether to knock or to try the handle. Footsteps down the hallway caught his attention. Humming accompanied each step, and he knew it was the castle's head maid, Mary, he believed her name was. If she saw him, it was unlikely that she would say anything and, even if she did, who was likely to take the word of such a lowly servant?

Deciding he didn't want to alarm her, it was best that the maid not see his true character right away. He knocked softly, hoping that Edana hadn't already retired for the evening.

She answered quickly, and he found himself unsure of how best to explain his unexpected arrival at her door. "Edana, how are ye this evening? I was passing by yer door and thought I would check in on ye."

He watched as her beady green eyes and pale blonde hair peered back at him, questioning without saying a word as to why he was there. She was shy, or at least she did a fine job of feigning shyness. He'd been around her enough, studied her enough to see how she behaved when she believed no one was watching, to know that the girl had far more fire and bite than she let on.

While many people who possessed the same fiery spirit were fueled by their immense passion for life, he recognized that Edana's fire came from a different source. Her fire raged out of an underlying malice for everything and everyone around her, something that she'd inherited from her father, no doubt. He knew she did her best to hide it, but he held the same feelings of malice for all those around him, and he could see it in her eyes even now as she looked back at him.

He smiled and glanced quickly to either side before speaking again. "May I come in? I doona wish to be seen outside your chamber this late in the evening."

Edana looked down at her feet and silently stepped away from the door, allowing Tormod entry into the room.

"What are ye doing here, Tormod? Ye shouldna be in this part of the castle." She spoke with her back toward him as she walked away, leaving him to stand just inside the doorway as she took a seat near the hearth.

Slowly, he moved to the seat across from her. When she didn't protest, he sat down by her side. "I wanted to see ye. I always want to see ye, but I've only just gathered the courage to do so."

"What? Why, I've never seen ye so much as look at me before." Her voice came out high and squeaky.

Tormod recognized that this was not part of her façade. She was genuinely surprised to hear his explanation. His confidence growing, he scooted in closer, reaching over to grasp her hand. "Aye. I've looked at ye many times before, lass, and I see ye now as well." He rubbed his thumb gently back and forth across the top of her hand until she moved away from his reach, standing as she pushed her hair from her face and opened the door so that he would leave.

"Ye canna mean it. I doona wish to be toyed with. 'Tis no enough that I just lost me father, and now I've been forced to live in the home of the very people who took him from me? Do ye wish to tease me as well? I willna allow it. Now, leave." She pointed toward the opening in the door and, as Tormod stood, he realized he'd just learned all he needed to know about the lass.

63

Not only did Edana hate most everyone around her, she also held herself in great contempt. Only someone with a very low sense of self-worth would immediately assume that a suitor at their door this late in the evening was there to belittle them. Edana's feelings toward herself would serve him well. It was easy to make self-loathing women fall in love. They would heedlessly throw their heart at the first suitor to ask for it, in the hopes of receiving the admiration they denied themselves.

Passing her on his way out the door, he paused quickly to steal a kiss. The whispery sigh that escaped her lips was not one of protest, and he smiled against her lips as he leaned forward to whisper in her ear. "I will never tease ye, Edana. I intend to make ye mine."

He didn't give her a chance to respond, turning quickly to make his leave. He knew his visit had been successful. He'd left the poor lass wanting more, with her heart beating wildly in her chest. In a week's time, she'd want no other man but him, of that he was sure.

* * *

Three Days Later

Arran rolled drowsily out of bed as he cursed Kip for creating so many tasks for him to complete in the stables that day. He knew it was unusual for someone in his position to work in the stables, but he didn't care. Keeping busy was the only thing keeping the drinking at bay and the pain in his heart at a safe distance.

He threw open the door to his bedchamber to see who felt the need to disturb him so late in the evening, and he had to blink several times to make sure he was seeing correctly when he saw Mary standing in his doorway.

"Mary? What are ye doing? Ye should've been in bed hours ago. Ye work too much as it is."

Mary waved a hand in dismissal at Arran's words as she stepped inside without waiting to be invited in. "I doona need ye telling me when I should be in bed, and I doona work too much. I work just the proper amount. 'Tis only that ye work too little that ye think anything more than that is too much."

"Ah. O'course ye are right, Mary." Arran knew better than to argue with her and so he simply smiled and crossed his arms as he prepared to hear what she had to say. "Now, what do ye need? Ye havena been in my bedchamber this late since I was a wee lad."

"Ye are right, and I see ye haven't changed yer bad habits at all. Ye still doona have enough common sense to check and make sure ye are properly clothed before ye invite company into yer room. For goodness sakes, cover yerself lad, I think ye have blinded me." She shielded her eyes dramatically as Arran glanced down at his entirely naked self.

"Ach, Christ, Mary! I'm verra sorry." Scrambling, he reached for something to cover himself, finally deciding to simply sit on the edge of the bed so that he could sit under the protection of fabric.

"Doona apologize, lad. 'Tis no like I havena seen a man naked before. Why, I used to clean that little backside of yers when ye were only a wee laddie."

Arran rolled his eyes, wishing Mary would spit out her news so that he could return to a peaceful slumber. "Ach, let's no talk about me backside. What's brought ye here?"

"Ah, right." Mary stopped grinning and faced him head on. "I'm verra worried about Edana."

"Aye? Why?" Arran was awake now. He'd been worried about the lass too, but he didn't understand why Mary would be. He straightened up in the bed, eager to hear her explanation.

"For the past three evenings, I have seen Tormod, the visitor who they all say is Ramsay's bastard nephew, sneaking into Lady Edana's room late at night. It isna proper for him to visit her after dark."

"Ye are right, it isna, but they are our guests, and I doona think 'tis our place to instruct them on how to behave themselves. Besides, I doubt he is doing anything to the lass she wouldna want him to." He believed his own words, but he couldn't deny how uncomfortable the thought made him. He wasn't jealous of Tormod. He didn't care about Edana in that way. But he had seen the lad interacting with some of his men and did not like the feeling he got around him.

"No, I doona think he is hurting her, Arran. I think he is using her so that he can become laird. Ye know that our visitors decided that whomever becomes laird should marry Edana. I believe he is trying to make her want to do just that, which would be fine except for I doona think Tormod is a good man. No even much better than Edana's father."

"Aye, I agree with ye, Mary. I doona like the lad either." Arran lay back on his bed, gathering the blankets to cover himself, drumming his fingers back and forth across his forehead as he tried to think of how to best proceed.

Only one plausible solution crossed his mind. Although the idea didn't thrill him, it was the only way he saw to keep his new friend from entering a horrible marriage. With no hope of his own true love coming back to him, what did it matter whom he married anyway? He sat up in the bed to tell Mary his plan. "I know what I shall do, Mary. We shall have a series of games to test the strength and leadership of all the men who enter. Whoever wins shall marry Edana and become laird of Kinnaird's old territory."

Mary drew her brows together, and Arran knew she did not yet understand his plan. "Aye, fine. But how do ye think ye shall get the Kinnaird Clan to agree to such an arrangement, and what if Tormod wins? That will do nothing to keep her from him."

"They will agree because they are all eager to name a new laird. If they do not, they will no longer have the hospitality of staying on our land. And Tormod willna win."

Mary's scrunched eyebrows rose in question. "And just how do ye know that? He's quite a strong looking lad."

"Tormod willna win because I plan to enter. I will win and marry Edana meself."

Chapter 11

Scotland – Present Day

I was unsure of how they'd convinced me to leave with them. It certainly meant losing another job, and I dinna have any other friends that could help me in obtaining another one once I returned to Edinburgh from our trip back into the country.

I continued to question my decision as I sat in the back of the small cramped car next to Bri's friend, Mitsy, who had thankfully settled down. I was sure that she thought us all mad. How could anyone not after hearing our story? All the same, she was no longer hysterical, and it was undeniable that she'd been in desperate need of a good night's sleep. She looked much better, even quite striking, with her long, red curls fixed nicely, no longer matted down by tears.

As we pulled up in front of the all-too-familiar inn near the castle, I realized that it was a potent mixture of fear and hope that had caused me to agree to stay here with Eoin for the next week. I'd sworn to myself that I wouldna return when I left, and I was terrified to do so now, but I was even more terrified of letting this opportunity slip away. I'd suspected last evening in the pub that there was more to Bri and Eoin's visit to this time than Bri's desire to finish some things she'd left undone. Somehow their visit involved me.

My suspicions were confirmed this morning when they'd asked me to leave town for a week to keep Eoin company and watch over him while Bri and Mitsy left for Mitsy's wedding. Eoin was more than capable of taking care of himself, especially if he was staying with Jerry and Gwendolyn, or was it Morna? None of us was sure of how to refer to the magical innkeeper anymore. Something remained that Eoin wanted to discuss with me, and my curiosity over that something was enough for me to leave my position in Edinburgh and run toward uncertainty once again.

It seemed likely that Eoin's news might only break my heart further and make me wish I'd remained in Edinburgh. He'd not said much about my father when I'd asked him. Perhaps he was ill or had discovered that I was gone. I hoped he hadn't. I wouldn't be able to bear the guilt of knowing I'd caused him such pain.

But what if it was something else? What if now that Eoin was married to someone else, Arran wanted me to return home to be with him? The thought made my stomach flutter excitedly, but just as quickly it turned to an uncomfortable churn as I realized what I knew must be true. Arran didn't want me to return. He probably didn't care that I was gone. If he did, he would have come here himself. He had far too much pride to allow his brother to make such a request of me.

The car had been parked for some time, and everyone else was unloading their belongings as I remained in the back seat, a familiar depression gliding over me as my latest realization drained away all the hope I'd had of Eoin's news being good.

After this week, I would return to the city, jobless once more, and I would start again.

My own reflection in the window to my left startled me, and I jumped as Bri lightly knocked against the window. "Come on inside, Blaire. They have food laid out for you and Eoin. Mitsy and

I have to be on our way to the airport. Our flight is in a couple of hours."

Doing my best to manage a smile, I apologized and joined the others inside. Shortly after, Bri and Mitsy drove away, leaving me to wallow in my nerves over what sad news Eoin had yet to share with me.

* * *

Austin, TX

As the song came to its end, Bri smiled at her dance partner as she pulled him in for a hug. "Thank you, Daniel. You're a wonderful dancer."

"It was my pleasure, dear." The man, forty years her senior, kissed her hand before showing her back to her seat. "And you're right. I am a wonderful dancer. If we'd only been able to go on our date, you would know that already."

Bri laughed as she sat down at the now empty table. All of those seated next to her were out on the dance floor. "My loss."

Daniel winked and tipped his head as he glided his way back onto the dance floor, no doubt looking for the next beautiful girl he could impress with his dance skills. Bri smiled to herself as she thought back on that night, which seemed like so many months ago, when she'd been set up on a blind date with Daniel. Her mother's sudden arrival had kept the date from ever beginning, but thinking back on the shock she'd experienced when first laying eyes on Daniel and the moments of awkwardness that had followed, Bri was reminded that she had some choice words to share with the groom.

It had been Mitsy's new husband, Brian, who'd arranged the blind date, and the lack of sense in the match did nothing to help

Bri's already questionable judgment of him. Tonight was not the time or place to chide the groom. With plans for her to return to Scotland and thereafter back to the seventeenth century the following day, Bri suspected she was just going to have to let this one slide.

Not that she would be able to find the groom to speak to him if she wanted. The last time she saw him had been at the beginning of the reception during the cutting of the cake and the first dance. Since then, Mitsy singly navigated the crowds of guests eager to congratulate the happy couple. From the beaming smile on Mitsy's face, it didn't seem that she'd taken note of her husband's absence.

Deciding she could go for a restroom break and perhaps for a little search and rescue mission for the groom, Bri stood and left the reception hall. Arriving at the women's restroom, she was met by the unfortunate staffer who had been dealt the task of cleaning up the puke of some tipsy wedding guest.

"Sorry. I don't think you want to come in here right now, but if you go to the end of the hall on the right, there's an office. If you enter, there's a bathroom connected to it on the other side. It's fine if you want to use it since you're part of the wedding party. I should have this mess cleaned up for the other guests shortly."

"Thank you, I think I'll do that."

Making her way down the hall, Bri found that her need to use the restroom lessened as she grew more apprehensive of who and what she would find in the office. A noise of a carnal nature came from behind the office door and, as she pressed her ear up against the wooden surface, she could hear the deep male voice, drenched in a thick Texas accent, urging the moaning woman in his company to say his name.

To Bri's dismay, the name the woman screamed was none other than Brian.

*   *   *

Bri fled the closed office door before her presence was discovered and quickly downed several glasses of champagne as she decided what she should do.

In the end, she'd watched her best friend, laughing and beaming as she moved through the reception hall, and knew that while she couldn't bring herself to tell Mitsy what she'd heard, she also didn't trust herself not to say anything.

She'd approached her dear friend on the dance floor, made her excuses claiming to be sick, and hugged her neck hard. Fighting back tears with a heavy heart, Bri hopped into a taxi that would take her back to her hotel.

Chances were, she'd never see her friend again, but she wanted to leave Mitsy the option of a new life if she decided she wanted it once she learned the truth about her louse of a husband. Mitsy would eventually, Bri was certain. She only wished that she could be here for her when she did.

Passing a post office on her right, Bri knocked on the plastic panel behind the taxi driver's head to get his attention. "Can we stop here just for a minute before continuing on to the airport? I just need to run inside and get a stamp. I need to put something in the mail before I leave."

"Sure thing. Meter's running."

Climbing out of the cab, Bri walked to buy the stamp, hoping with every footstep that if Mitsy needed it, she would be able to believe the words she'd written inside.

Chapter 12

Scotland - 1646

Tormod's eyes locked with hers as Edana watched him rise from yet another victory, this time in the sword competition. She shivered beneath her clothes at the tingly rush that cascaded over her. She was in love, she could say so without hesitation. Only a week ago, her future had seemed bleak, wrought with uncertainty and a plan for vengeance that she didn't know how to carry out on her own. Now, with Tormod by her side, happiness no longer seemed so impossible.

He loved her as well and although he'd yet to tell her so, she knew it by the way he treated her. She'd felt she could trust him instantly and had quickly told him about her true feelings toward the Conalls and her desire to destroy them. She'd expected him to reprimand her, tell her how wrong she was to think that way, but instead, he'd expressed his own hatred. Together they'd plotted all they could do to destroy the powerful family once they were married and Tormod was laird.

Now, all that stood in their way was the final round of the so-called games that Arran had dreamed up. She found it sickening that her clansmen had so easily agreed to trust her future to a contest. Only a group of men would be so thoughtless. When Arran put the idea to the clan, she'd openly voiced her misgivings on the proposal. With the men eager to return home and with no better

73

solutions themselves, they all boisterously agreed to Arran's plan, throwing aside all thought or concern for her own feelings.

The only thing that had calmed her was Tormod's reassurance that he would win the competition for her. And she believed that he would. He was close to doing so already. Only one more person would Tormod have to best, and that was by far the most surprising revelation that came out of Arran's idea.

Not only had Arran stood before her clansmen suggesting how to choose their leader, a move that she saw as highly inappropriate and insulting to their intelligence, but he had also asked the clansmen to grant him permission to enter the contest as well. The people of their clan had worked and lived together for decades and, in time, they would have been more than capable of solving their problem of leadership on their own.

He moved into a lengthy speech where he vowed that if he were to win, as he obviously thought he would, he would be a fair and strong leader, unlike Edana's father. Each word was another dagger destroying any fond memories her clansmen might have had of her father. Each word stoked the fire of hatred that burned within her for Arran and all of the Conalls, each of them so self-assured in the righteousness of their actions.

To her utter dismay, her clansmen had wholeheartedly welcomed him for entrance, many boasting that they would be rooting for him to win, few even questioning the purpose of the competition. Why not just name Arran laird now?

What a fool Arran was. He thought he could trick her into liking him with his kind words and feigned concern for her wellbeing. 'Twas even more foolish still for him to have such utter confidence in his ability to win her and her territory as his prize.

Tormod would never allow it, and if he did, Edana was certain she would kill herself before marrying a Conall.

With archery being the only competition left, Edana stood to go in search of her beloved. She wanted to wish him luck and perhaps steal a kiss from the man she would soon call her husband.

* * *

Tormod stood in the corner of his tent, hunched over as he carefully examined each of his arrows looking for any inconsistency, any warp in the wood, that would impact his shot. Archery was his strength, but he knew Arran was masterful with a bow as well. He could leave no room for error if he wanted to become laird. It was within his grasp. He would be laird by nightfall. Then in a few short weeks, his marriage to Edana would be bound with consummation. He could finally end the dreadful task of pretending to like the disgusting wretch.

The rustle of fabric to his left caused him to spin, eager to see who was entering. He'd asked to be left alone so that he could concentrate in silence before the last challenge. His sister entered, and he was not surprised that it would be she who gave no credence to his wishes.

"Fia, why are ye here?"

She ignored his question and moved over to his arrows, grabbing one as she raised it in question to him. "Do ye think ye can win?"

The question angered him, and he ripped the arrow out of her hand before continuing. "Aye. I can and I will. Do ye no think so?"

She shook her head in denial. "No, I do think that ye can. 'Tis only I doona think that ye should."

75

Tormod couldn't believe what she was saying to him. She was just as eager for their family to gain a place of leadership once again. She too had been denied her birthrights because of the sins of their parents. "Why the hell would ye say such a thing, Fia? 'Tis within our grasp now. We will finally be allowed in the castle that should have always been our home."

"Aye and we shall be, but doona do it today, brother. The people of our clan want Arran to win today. If ye defeat him, they will only resent ye. Claim the lairdship in a way that will earn the respect of our people."

Tormod shook his head, confused and angry at his sister's suggestion. "Aye, and how would I claim it once Arran is named laird?"

"Ye watch him, stay close to him, and find a truth that ye can distort into a believable lie. Make the people believe that their precious laird has perpetrated whatever crime ye decide to make him guilty of. Then it will be much easier for ye to take over as laird. Ye will have earned the trust of our people, and ye may be able to get rid of Edana in the process as well. I know ye doona wish to be married to the lass."

Tormod paced the room, shaken by the thought of giving up everything within his grasp. He tightened his jaw as he turned to send his sister away. "Ye are right. I doona wish to marry Edana, but there are other ways to dispose of the lass once I am laird. I willna give this up, and if ye wish to be moved to the castle as well once I am laird, ye willna ask it of me again. Now leave at once."

He turned his back as he waited for his sister to leave, tightening his fists as her last words caused him to vibrate with rage.

"As ye wish, but ye will regret this Tormod, and ye will see that I was right."

* * *

Each of them must shoot ten arrows. Tormod had just shot his seventh. As Arran drew his seventh and sent it soaring into the center of the target, Tormod didn't miss the roar of his clansmen. Their scores tied once again. With each perfect shot of his own, Arran matched it. Currently it seemed that they would have to go well beyond ten shots to declare a winner.

Drawing his own arrow, Tormod released another flawless shot, quickly turning to take in the crowd that remained mostly silent. His sister had been right. There was no denying the well wishes of his own clansmen lay with his rival. It would be a difficult lairdship if he took over as leader without the support of his people behind him.

Edana would be furious, but he knew that he could comfort her with his lies. He could make her work with him, and perhaps it would be even easier to destroy Arran if he had an ally that shared Arran's bed.

With Arran sending another perfect shot, Tormod drew his bow and jerked his body at the last minute so that his arrow went flying wildly to the side, missing the target completely.

He would allow Arran to be laird for now, but it would be short-lived. Tormod vowed to contemplate a dozen ways to destroy the doomed Conall.

Chapter 13

Scotland – Present Day

Bri was due back to arrive at the inn today, and I still had no idea what Eoin wished to speak with me about. The week had passed in anything but silence as we spent most of our time listening to stories told by Jerry and Morna, whom finally had asked that we call her by her real name.

She was a vivid storyteller, and we all enjoyed listening to the adventure stories of Eoin's father, Alasdair, and my own father when they were growing up. 'Twas a pleasure to watch Eoin discover the aunt he hardly remembered and had envisioned in his mind as a very different woman than she actually was. Her spells and magic were just a small part of the lively, funny, warm woman, and 'twas easy to see why Alasdair had adored his sister so much when many of those around them feared her.

'Twas the first morning Eoin and I had spent alone together. Jerry and Morna had left earlier to visit a neighbor, but I was quite certain the closest thing they had to a neighbor was the castle itself. I suspected they'd left to allow us time to talk.

We sat across from each other in the living room as Eoin tried to busy himself with the television remote, randomly pushing the buttons, watching with fascination as the pictures changed on the screen. I sat silently for a few moments, knowing that my impatience was about to burst forth if he dinna set the remote down and start talking soon. Still, I knew my own fascination with the oddities of this century and so tried to be understanding.

"Eoin. Will ye please turn it off? It's time for ye to tell me why ye and Bri asked me to come here."

He dinna look at me immediately, instead staring at the remote as he searched for a way to stop the moving pictures. I reached over and pushed on the red button, taking it from his hands as the television ceased its movement.

Rising up, he situated himself more comfortably on the couch and crossed his arms as he looked up at me. "Aye, I suppose 'tis time. I should tell ye beforehand that this wasna me idea. And I'm no too pleased with Bri for leaving me here to ask this of ye, all alone. She knows more of this than I."

Why would Bri know more about anything than Eoin? She'd been there only a short period of time, and while I was still adjusting to the many differences of modern day life, I was sure she was still adjusting to the loss of modern conveniences, as well. "Just get on with it, Eoin. I doona care which one of ye tells me, I'm only anxious to know. Ye have left me waiting for the past week."

"I know and I'm sorry. I'm only unsure of how to explain this to ye." He paused as he cleared his throat, searching for a way to delay explanation even further.

"Eoin, if ye doona wish for me to cause ye physical harm, it would best serve ye to tell me right away." I leaned forward, placing my elbows on my knees and rested my head on my clenched fists, doing my best to look as threatening as possible.

His hesitation ended as he spoke very quickly, obviously nervous. "Bri seems to believe that ye were in love with Arran, and that is why ye left. Ye dinna want to marry me, and ye couldna

79

marry him, so ye decided to stay here. She believes that Arran is in love with ye, as well."

I stiffened as I sat, every muscle clenching as if they desired to strangle me. I was suddenly breathless, and my heart pounded painfully at the hope-filled words I'd stopped allowing myself to imagine I would ever hear. "Why?" I had to pause and cough as my throat suddenly filled with cobwebs. "What reason would Bri have for believing such a thing?"

"Arran's behavior as of late. He has never been a stranger to the drink, but he has been drinking more than ever lately. And I havena seen him in the company of another woman in a long time. I do admit that he seems rather sad, but until Bri mentioned it, I dinna put it up to being from a broken heart."

It was hard for me to imagine Arran drinking more than he already did. The very day Arran had sent me away from him, he'd said he would soon share his bed with another. If he had not, perhaps Eoin was right. It filled me with a hope I could scarcely allow myself to believe without proof of his feelings.

"Has he told ye that he loves me, Eoin? If he did, surely he would have told his own brother. Ye have always been his closest friend, and now that ye are married to Bri, what would have been the harm in him expressing his feelings to ye?" Rising from my crouched position on my knees, I stood, feeling the need to move about the room, the rush of mixed feelings making the space suddenly seem too small.

"No, lass, he hasna told me, but I think Bri may be right. There was something that happened shortly after our wedding that should have warned me of his feelings for ye."

I paused in front of the fireplace, keeping my back toward him, reluctant to allow him to see my eyes slowly filling with tears. "Aye? What happened?"

"There was a small fire set after the wedding that I was required to attend to, leaving Bri alone in our bedchamber. When I returned, I found Bri pinned to the wall outside of our bedchamber, with her dress falling below her breasts and Arran kissing her quite madly."

I spun, my desire to hide my emotions suddenly forgotten. "What?"

"Aye, lass. I hit Arran, and he fell to the ground unconscious, and I threw Bri in the dungeon."

I interrupted, unable to stop myself. "Ye threw me in the dungeon? On our wedding night!"

Eoin looked down at the floor. Someone else had clearly already reprimanded him for his actions. "I dinna throw ye in the dungeon, did I? It was Bri, but I doona wish to talk about it. It is no the point."

"Aye, fine." I smiled at him briefly, urging him to continue.

"Arran blamed his actions on having too much to drink, but no man, no matter how drunk, would kiss a woman in such a familiar way unless he'd already done so many times before."

He quieted, and it was my turn to feel guilty. Regardless of how happy Eoin was with his new bride now, it was I who had been promised to him by my father, and I'd been unfaithful to him by the feelings I'd held for his brother.

"I'm sorry, Eoin. Me behavior was disgraceful, and ye did nothing to deserve me betrayal of ye."

"Ach, think nothing of it, lass. Ye and I were no meant for a marriage together. All I want now is for me brother to be happy and for ye to find happiness as well. If that is something that the two of ye may find together, ye have me every blessing. If ye still love him, Blaire, we'd like ye to return home with us."

"Do ye truly believe he still loves me?" The words were already bubbling to the front of my mouth, but I wanted one more reassurance before agreeing to come home.

"Aye, I do. And Bri is certain of it. She's a wise woman. I've yet to find her wrong in anything."

"Then aye. I will come."

"Well done, Eoin."

Bri's voice in the doorway startled us both, and we stood to welcome her back.

"I knew you could convince her to come without me. Now, let's head to the castle. We've all been gone too long. Mother and Mary will both be in a tizzy."

* * *

1646

The wedding was arranged quickly. Only three days following his victory, Arran stood next to Edana in front of the crowd filled with his new clansmen. His brother would certainly be surprised upon his arrival back at home to find that he had moved away and now was a married laird. But Arran was sure he would be happy to have the security of having a guaranteed ally in the place of Ramsay's former territory.

Their ceremony was coming to a close and, while he repeated the words asked of him, each promise made was made to the woman who owned his heart, not to the woman who stood beside him now. As he closed his eyes to kiss his new bride, it was Blaire's face that he saw leaning into him.

Chapter 14

Tormod scooted further up the rock upon which he sat along the hillside cliff in an effort to avoid yet another spray from the ocean as the waves crashed upon the rocks. It was a cold evening and the water was freezing, just another reason he was thankful he and his fellow clansmen did not live in such close proximity to the ocean.

Edana was supposed to meet him here. She'd promised him right before the wedding ceremony that she would, but as the sun dropped lower and lower over the horizon, he began to question her loyalty to him.

While she'd spoken venomous words about Arran and his family, Tormod had seen Edana be quite friendly with Arran on more than one occasion. As the sun made its final bow against the horizon and night spread itself over the sky above him, Tormod stood to leave. Just as he stood, he heard Edana's voice behind him.

"I'm sorry. I was delayed. What are we to do, Tormod? It will be difficult for us to meet now that I am married to him."

He couldn't have cared less about the tears she shed as she sat down next to him, burying her head in her hands as she wept. If he was to keep Edana's interest and loyalty, he knew he must show her sympathy.

"Come here, lass. I doona wish to see ye cry. Yer marriage changes nothing. We shall be together as often as we can, and soon enough I will be laird."

Edana lifted her head. With great difficulty, Tormod kept his face from showing his displeasure at her red, tear-stained face.

"How can that be? The men love Arran. They are glad to have him as laird and they willna take well to someone trying to take away his position."

"Nay, they willna just now," Tormod assured her. "In time we shall find a way to change their opinion of him."

"How?" Edana collapsed into a fit of sobs once more.

Tormod stood, incapable of soothing the lass any further. "I doona know yet, but ye shall be spending much time with Arran from now on. Watch him, find something in his behavior that we can twist into an untruth, some way in which we can claim he did something he did not and make others believe that it is so. It may take some time."

Edana sniffled, looking up and breathing deeply as if trying to stop her tears. "Aye, I shall do me best. Tell me, Tormod, I need to know, I fear 'tis the only thing that shall get me through every horrible moment I must spend with Arran. Do ye love me? Would ye wish to be with me even if it would no make ye laird?"

She stood and moved next to him. He pulled her in close, wrapping his arms around her as he kissed her on the top of her head. "Aye, o'course I do. I love ye as much as I've ever loved anyone."

The second part of what he'd said was true, not that he'd ever loved anyone, save himself and perhaps his sister. The first, his declaration of love, was the lie, but it had slipped out easily. And perhaps he did love the lass a bit. At least, he loved what she would do for him and the power that would be delivered into his hands with her assistance.

Squeezing her once more in farewell, he pushed her away and waved her off to the castle.

"'Tis best that ye go. Yer new husband will be searching for ye, and we doona need to give him reason to be suspicious. I shall seek ye out after we have all arrived back home in a few weeks, after ye are both settled into yer castle."

"I shall miss ye every moment that I am no with ye, Tormod."

After she left him, he sat down on the rocks laughing quietly to himself. The lass was a fool to believe that he would care for her. He needed to find a way to destroy Arran soon. He didn't know how much more of the pathetic lass he could take.

*   *   *

Early the next morning before the sun had risen, Arran snuck out of his room to retrieve his new bride from his late-mother's bedchamber. All castle workers and wedding guests, Mary being the one exception, assumed the newly married bride and groom had spent their first night of marriage together, and that was just the way he wanted to keep it. It wouldn't do if it was found out that neither of them had wanted to consummate their marriage.

After their wedding, Edana had briefly disappeared. When Arran finally found her, the marks of freshly run tears stained her face. He'd rushed her away to his bedchamber to comfort her, but she'd pulled away claiming her tears were caused by her fears of their wedding night.

While he suspected all new brides approached their wedding night with some anxiety, Edana's reaction seemed to be caused by more than just nerves. Arran had already suspected that Edana's father had harmed the lass in some way, but her apprehension for their wedding night only solidified his suspicions of just how monstrous Ramsay Kinnaird had been.

The lass's fears aside, Arran was not eager to consummate the marriage either, his feelings for her being only of a platonic nature. Instead, he'd not questioned her, not pushed the ritual they were both expected to complete, but ushered her quietly down the hall to the safety of her own room.

Arran knew the consummation would have to be completed, but that could come in time, when the bonds of friendship were a little stronger between the two of them. For now, he would simply collect her from her room, and together they would make their way to the stables where they would meet with his new clansmen so they could begin their journey to the new Conall Castle.

* * *

"What do you mean they didn't consummate their marriage? How on earth would you know that, Mary? Goodness, I know that you're nosy, but I didn't know you were a peeping Tom. What did you do, cut a peep hole into Arran's bedroom?" Adelle laughed at her own wit. Mary had to refrain from whopping the woman on the nose. Bri, she loved, but it was going to take her more time to adjust to the loud-mouthed, say-anything ways of her mother. "I doona know what a 'peeping Tom' is, but I doona believe I like what ye are suggesting. O'course I dinna spy on them. I know they dinna consummate the marriage because Arran had me prepare his mother's room for Edana to stay in. They dinna spend the night

87

together." Mary continued kneading the dough as her nosy kitchen visitor sat across from her watching.

"No! Why? It's because Bri was right, isn't it? He does still love Blaire. I knew we should've stopped that marriage, Mary! Perhaps, it's not too late to do something. If they've not consummated it, it's not actually binding, is it?"

"I doona know why they dinna spend the night together, but aye, I do believe Bri was right. But it doesna matter, there is nothing we can do because everyone else believes the marriage is consummated, and we are no going to tell them anything different. Do ye understand me?"

"Why? We must. Bri is going to kill us both when she gets back here with Blaire, and we've let Arran run off and marry somebody else."

Mary threw her hands up in exasperation sending a cloud of flour soaring into the air. "What do ye think she would have expected us to do to stop him? Arran listens to no one, especially when it is someone trying to stop him from doing something foolish. If Blaire returns, which I doona think she will, she will overcome it in time. I doona like it for either of them, but both have made their own choices. 'Tis no our place to meddle."

"Not our place? That's what mothers do, Mary. And regardless of your position here in the castle, you know as well as I do that you are just as much a mother to those lads as their real mother was. They were young when they lost her, and you've been there for them and loved them since they were babes."

Mary couldn't help but smile. Adelle was right, she loved those boys as if they were her own. Movement in the doorway caused her to glance up from the heap of dough and, as Kip approached her with a letter extended in her direction, Mary turned to dip her hands into a bucket of water to cleanse them of the flour.

"What is it?" Shaking them dry, Mary reached for the parchment in her husband's hand.

"I doona know. Saw the lad riding up so I stopped him and told him I'd take it here meself. It's addressed to Eoin but, seeing as both lads are gone, I expect that 'tis ye that should open it."

"Aye, o'course." Mary broke the seal and unfolded the parchment. She shook her head as she read the words. "It wouldna do for Old Mary to have one day of rest. One day with both of the lads gone for me to rest and pretend that I live a life of leisure. Nay, such a small wish is too much for me to receive." She paused and pointed at her husband. "Kip, ye will need to gather every one near us to help get the castle in order. We doona only have to clean up the mess our guests left us, but we have a new batch of visitors arriving. Lady McMillan and her three sons arrive here the day after next."

Chapter 15

The Castle Formerly Known As Kinnaird

The first evening Edana spent at what would now be considered Conall Castle since her father's death, she felt his presence everywhere. The remains of his hatred, his abuse, his insanity weighing down upon her, taunting her, pleading with her to finish what he'd started.

Her father had given his life to defeat the Conalls, and it had all been for nothing. His worst nightmare had come true. A Conall now led, and his only daughter was now married to one as well.

Edana moved through the hallways haunted by the memories of her childhood, a childhood filled with fear, filled with manipulation, filled with abuse. Now that her father was gone, she wanted to move on, to live a happier life than the one he had provided her. But with her father's plan for the Conalls' demise unfinished, she knew her father's presence would remain over her, tempting her to the madness that he'd surrendered to. The only hope she had of finding peace with him, of ending his control on her life, was to finish what he'd begun.

The Conalls were too confident, too powerful, and too trusting for their own good. Those reasons alone would have been enough to make her hate them, but their defeat of her father had chained her to him. Until she was released from his hold, she would never be able to find the happiness she knew she would find with Tormod.

Arran had already retired for the evening in her father's old room. While he'd given her permission to spend the night elsewhere, Edana knew it was best not to put off the inevitable. The marriage had to be consummated, considered invalid otherwise. She knew the servants of this castle well enough to know that they would speak if she did not visit her husband's room.

She couldn't allow questions to arise about the marriage. She needed to do as Tormod had bid her, to spend time with Arran and find a weakness they could exploit to his demise.

Edana paced back and forth, pausing in front of Arran's door with each passing. She was certain what must follow would be the worst moments of her life. Thinking of it brought back flashes of horror she did her best to push away. This would be different than the times before. She was older. No longer a child. And she was now choosing this of her own free will.

Tormod had yet to touch her beyond a swift kiss during their stolen moments together. Still, she knew the scars of her past would have caused her to be just as frightened as she was now if it were he she must bed rather than a man she didn't love.

She could only hope Arran wouldn't notice the lack of blood. It could mean the end of their marriage if he did. For many men it would, but she suspected Arran would be different. Just another reason he could be easily defeated. He was caring and kind, and that made him weak.

Gathering her courage, she glanced at her reflection in a piece of armory hanging on the wall. Pushing her hair out of her face, she pinched her cheeks to bring up a blush. Before she could change her mind, Edana knocked on her husband's door.

* * *

The dark castle lacked access to sunlight, unlike his old home that was filled with such great light. Not only the structure itself made his new home dark, but the scarred remnants of Ramsay's legacy was etched deep into every piece of furniture and tapestry. Arran wouldn't allow it to stay that way for long.

He planned to turn the castle into a place of joy, a place their children would enjoy for many, many years. A place where his new clansmen could rest assured that they were now represented by a fair and just leader rather than the abomination who'd ruled over them before.

He'd been away in the bedchamber for hours composing a letter to send to his brother, hoping to provide him with more explanation on his surprising choices as of late. He had just finished and was preparing to retire when he heard a soft knock on the door.

Glancing down at himself, a new habit he'd formed thanks to Mary, and finding himself decently clothed, he went to open the door.

Edana stood before him, draped in her nightgown, hair down and pushed back behind her ears. She held a candle which shook lightly in her hands, a sure sign of her nerves, and Arran knew instantly why she'd come to him.

He invited her in, but his insides twisted. He was sure his former self, the Arran before Blaire, would think him mad, but he still found himself rather uneager to bed his new wife.

Despite his misgivings, it would be impossible for him to deny her. He knew what courage it took for her to come to him, and it was an act that must be performed. It was the only way to secure his place as laird, to legitimize their marriage, and he knew that Edana was offering him a kindness by recognizing that fact and offering herself to him without his bidding.

But there was no need to hurry into the act right away. He suspected that she would be much like a frightened animal. If he wished her not to bolt, he would need to take his time and move gently.

He moved to a table near his doorway and poured her some wine, extending it in her direction as he moved to stand away from her, leaning his back against the wall.

"How are ye this evening, Edana? I am surprised to find ye here so late. Is there something the matter?" He needed to be certain he was right about her reasons for coming to his room.

She downed the wine quickly, and Arran couldn't keep his eyes from widening in surprise.

"All is fine with me room. 'Tis the same as it has always been."

She extended the cup back to him, and he quickly refilled it before resuming his place against the wall. "Ye know that ye are welcome in here, Edana, but might I ask? Is there a particular reason for yer visit?"

She sat her wine down and moved toward him. He tensed all over, unsure of how to proceed. She leaned into him, gently kissing him on the cheek and whispered softly as she lingered near his mouth. "I think ye know, Arran. I'm no longer afraid of ye."

She kissed him then, softly, slowly, doing her best to seduce him, but he could feel the soft tremble in her lips, and gently lacing his hands with her own, he pulled away from her.

"I doona believe ye, lass. I can tell ye are frightened by the way ye are shaking, but that is fine. 'Tis no an uncommon thing for a woman to be quite scared when she is unaccustomed to sharing her bed with a man. But ye do know that this is something we must do, aye? 'Tis why ye have come." She looked up at him, her eyes hesitant, and his sympathy for her made his heart ache.

"Aye. Ye are now me husband, and 'tis yer right to have me. It would be improper for me to deny ye."

He moved his right hand and brought it up to her face, cupping it gently as he tried to reassure her with his eyes. "Nay, lass. 'Tis no me right, but it shall be me pleasure, and I am honored that ye offer me the gift of yerself. Please know that I would never hurt ye, lass, and I will never do anything ye doona want me to. Doona ever be afraid to tell me no. Ye doona belong to me, lass. Ye belong to none but yerself. Doona ever forget that or let anyone make ye believe differently."

Arran moved toward her, pulling her in close so that he could place his mouth to hers. He slowly warmed her lips with soft, feather-light kisses. He wanted it to be her choice, something she wanted of him. It would be hard enough for him to be the lover to her that she deserved, the image of Blaire burned forever in his heart, but he feared the task would be impossible if he knew Edana offered herself to him out of duty.

As he continued to press gently against her lips, asking her but not partaking of her until she granted him permission, her mouth suddenly opened to him, matching his rhythm as he increased the intensity of his kiss.

Accepting her own invitation, Arran turned, putting out the fire and candles, gently guiding her to the bed as blackness engulfed the room.

Neither of them could see the other as they surrendered, losing themselves in a visionless passion. They lay together through the night, each of them seeing the image of another in their minds.

Chapter 16

Adelle rushed frantically around the castle ensuring that each job placed on Mary's task list was completed perfectly. She knew as much as anybody that Conall Castle was Mary's ship to run, but with the quick succession of guests leaving and new visitors arriving today, the mess around the castle was more than even the great Mary could accomplish on her own.

Adelle knew that she gave the old, uptight drill sergeant a hard time. Truth was, the woman simply amazed her. Adelle suspected that despite her crusty exterior Mary was pretty fond of her as well. Seeing the stress that the news of their arriving-any-minute guests had brought to her, Adelle wanted to do all she could to help her new friend.

Satisfied that the castle sparkled enough for even the most discerning eyes, she followed her nose down to the kitchen, the salty smell of stew causing her stomach to growl.

She'd expected to find Mary bent over a large pot, stirring and seasoning away until whatever concoction she'd worked up for the evening meal was just to her satisfaction, but instead she found the kitchen unmanned. The room was completely empty save for the loaves of bread laid out and the bubbling, steaming, saliva-building stew warming over the fire. Too much for Adelle's over-eager stomach to take. Turning her head in each direction to confirm that she truly was alone, she tip-toed into the kitchen.

She was doing Mary a favor by attending to the food herself. Who knew what sort of contaminants or poisons could have been slipped into the pot while Mary was away? The only proper thing to do was to test it herself, to make sure that it was safe for the consumption of their guests.

Reaching up toward one of the room's many shelves, Adelle grabbed for a wooden bowl that she swiftly dipped into the steaming stew and filled it to the brim with the stew's yummy goodness.

She seated herself with her back to the doorway. She didn't want to get caught red-handed if someone decided to come down into the kitchen. She glanced around for a utensil to eat her stolen prize. Finding nothing, she quickly brushed her fingertips on the hem of her dress and, judging them clean enough for the time being, dipped her fingers inside to pick up a juicy slab of meat.

Mary had outdone herself with this one. Each bite seemed more delicious than the last, and Adelle lost herself as she ravenously chowed down on Mary's creation. She would forever be grateful for the rapid metabolism she'd inherited from her own mother. Without it, Adelle knew without doubt that she would weigh three hundred pounds as opposed to her slight, size two frame.

When she heard voices coming from the floor above her, she stopped her prize-winning chow-down. Straining to listen, she could hear Mary's voice welcoming the guests. Knowing her appearance would be quickly expected, Adelle swallowed the last piece of meat whole and raised the bowl to her mouth, tipping it high so that she could drink the last of the stew.

Shoving the bowl back onto the shelf, she would do her best to remember to come back and clean it. She took the stairs two at a time, hoping she would be able to greet their new guests before Mary showed them to their rooms.

When she made it to the top of the stairs, she paused quickly to catch her breath. Finally moving with as much grace as she could muster, she stepped into the main entranceway to greet their guests.

* * *

"What did I tell ye about getting into the kitchen when I'm no in there? No one eats before mealtime." Mary ground out the words to Adelle between clenched teeth as soon as they'd seen their guests to their rooms and they began making their way down to the kitchen together.

Adelle's eyes widened as she turned to glance guiltily in Mary's direction. "I have no idea what you are talking about."

"Aye, ye do. Doona lie to me. Look!" Mary moved in front of her, effectively blocking Adelle from taking another step down the small staircase. Taking her by surprise, she reached up and brushed a finger on either side of Adelle's mouth, pulling them away to reveal light brown globs of stew.

Adelle sat down on the step behind her and threw her forehead into the palm of her hand.

"Oh, no. Please don't tell me. Tell me I didn't spend all that time visiting with Lady McMillan and her sons with that goopy mess all over my face."

Mary chuckled loudly, obviously pleased with herself as Adelle continued to sink further into a state of mortification.

"Aye, ye did. I canna believe ye dinna notice them staring at yer mouth. I think poor Baodan almost wiped it for ye more than

98

once, but he never worked up the nerve." Mary collapsed into hearty laughter once again.

Adelle stood and stormed off in front of her, continuing to make her own way down the stairs. "Why didn't you tell me? I don't think I've ever been this embarrassed in my entire life."

"Why dinna I tell ye? Because that's what ye deserve for sticking yer mouth in things that ye know ye are no meant to. And as wild as ye are, 'tis certain ye have embarrassed yerself far worse than this before."

"That is completely and totally beside the point." Adelle reached the kitchen first, and before Mary could protest, retrieved her used bowl and filled it up with stew once more. "And don't you say a word about me getting another bowl."

Mary smiled and laughed once more. "Aye, go ahead and eat all ye like, Adelle. Why, the look on their faces. Well, I havena laughed that hard in quite a long time. Yer foolishness has brought me great joy. I no longer care what ye eat."

* * *

Present Day

"Ye look a fair mess, Eoin. Do ye think that we could have Morna take a photo of ye in that outfit that we could take back with us? I think it could provide the rest of us with much entertainment." I smiled as Eoin rewarded me with a quick but vicious glare as he moved uncomfortably in the restraint of his denim jeans.

Bri had been weary of taking him back to the spell room dressed the way he'd arrived. While Eoin was far too tall to fit into any of Kip's clothes, Morna had been able to come up with a pair of jeans, tennis shoes, and a dark blue sweater that fit Eoin perfectly. I suspected casting up clothes was a simple task compared to making it possible for people to travel through time.

Morna turned to address all of us as we gathered in the entranceway of her home preparing to make our exit. "I shall miss ye all dearly, but remember that ye can find me if ye need too, aye?"

We nodded in unison, and Bri stepped forward to squeeze Morna's neck. "Thank you. And you'll help her if she needs it? I mean, you remember what Mitsy looked like right?"

Morna hugged her tightly and patted her on the back in comfort. "Aye, o'course we do. The inn will always be available to yer friend to find if she needs it. The spell room as well. Now, ye best all be on yer way so that ye can sneak into the room before they lock the castle up for the evening."

Bri had remained unusually quiet since she'd arrived from her trip and, after the words I'd just listened to between her and Morna, I suspected it had something to do with her friend Mitsy. I would have to remember to ask her about it once we were home and things were settled.

We each said our goodbyes and, within the hour, found ourselves in the spell room once more. The spell was easily cast. As we clung to one another, the all-too-familiar pain ripped through us.

We disappeared into dust together.

Chapter 17

1646

Our re-entry into the past brought with it the expected headache and a short moment of confusion. It seemed to take me a little longer to recover from the travel as I glanced over at Eoin and Bri who seemed to be back to their usual selves.

"I doona care how much ye like the way my bum looks in jeans, I willna wear them again. As soon as I can pry them off me, I shall burn them until every last scrap has disappeared."

"Don't you dare! You don't have to wear them all the time, but for God's sake, don't burn them! That's the only set of modern male clothing we have. What if somebody else ever needs to go forward again?"

"We are all here now, I doona have any plans of going forward ever again."

"Neither do I, Eoin, but seriously, quit being such a child. You're not going to burn them. Just take them off. I'm folding them up and storing them with our clothing," Bri demanded. My vision no longer blurred and my headache already receded, I slipped into a dark corner of the room to change without Eoin seeing and joined in agreement with Bri. "She is right, Eoin. I doona know why ye would want to burn them. I would love to stay in me jeans forever. I doona wish to go back to wearing me old clothes at all."

101

Bri smiled in my direction as she extended a dress for me to slip on in replacement of my modern clothes. "Don't worry. You can still wear them some. Sometimes I sneak down here just to put them on. If we can ever get Eoin and Arran to leave us alone in the castle, we will put them on and just strut around all day and shock the bejeezus out of every person we see. It will be such great fun!"

I laughed, twisting to the side so that Bri could help me with the laces. "Aye, I look forward to the day. I hope me hair grows fast. Being back here, it suddenly feels too short."

"Doona worry about that, lass. 'Tis no that short, but as to the clothing, ye both would be fools to do such a thing. If the wrong people were to see ye dressed in such a way, they'd have ye burnt for witchcraft, and they wouldna all together be lying. Now, let's go and make our return known." Eoin turned and left, leaving Bri and me alone in the small spell room.

Bri turned to follow her husband, but I reached out and placed a hand on her arm to stop her. "Bri, do ye think Arran will be pleased that I am here? I'm quite nervous to see him." She reached up and squeezed me hand.

"I really think he will. Don't be nervous. We will look for Mary and my mother first. I don't expect Arran will be in the castle anyhow. He spends most of his time either in the stables with Kip or drinking in the village."

Taking a deep breath, I followed her out of the spell room. Nerves were senseless. I knew they would do nothing to change the outcome of whatever reunion was about to occur.

* * *

102

The room grew warm as Eoin, Bri, Adelle, Mary, and myself sat surrounding the work table in Mary's kitchen. That's where we'd found Adelle and Mary, and the excitement of their welcome had quickly become a muddled chaos as everyone seemed to speak at once.

Eventually we'd sat together, each person eager to hear a different set of news. I feigned attention for most of the time as I anxiously awaited the answer to one question I was too afraid to ask myself.

When Eoin finally said it out loud, my entire body went numb, pricked with a thousand pins, at Mary's response.

"He isna here, Eoin. All of Kinnaird's clansmen have left, and his former territory shall now be known as a Conall territory as well. He is laird there now, and he has married Edana."

"What?" Bri's voice questioned her, her voice shrill and panicked as she glanced at me uncomfortably.

"Aye. I'm afraid 'tis true. They left here only a few nights ago." Mary cast her eyes downward.

I could tell that she was not pleased by the news she had to share with us. I was helpless in discerning my own feelings, the excited hope and bright future I'd been imagining suddenly dying like the candle I found myself staring into. At least he wasn't here to tell me this himself. The words from his mouth would have felt like rejection all over again. Perhaps now I could simply leave, return home to my father whom I was sure would be more than happy to marry me off to another man of his choosing.

"Why didn't you stop him?" Bri changed the direction of her words and was now addressing her mother.

"There was nothing we could do, Bri. You made us swear not to tell him where'd you actually gone. We couldn't give him a good reason not to marry her without telling him what the two of you were up to."

"I don't care. That was the one reason good enough to break your promise." Bri looked as if she was on the brink of tears herself.

Wanting to stop her, I let the one question at the forefront of my own mind slip out. "Does he love her?"

Silence rewarded my question as I watched Adelle and Mary share knowing glances with one another, both unsure of how to give me an answer.

"No." Bri answered, but both Mary and Adelle nodded in agreement.

Somehow it seemed that both women thought that it would be even more devastating for me to learn he'd married if he was not in love with Edana. And perhaps it was.

For if Arran had married for love, I would have been left with no choice but to move on with my life. To grow old, certain in the knowledge that there was never any hope that it would be me who spent my life at his side.

But knowing that he dinna love her, that would be more difficult for me to heal from. I would live every day wondering, hoping and wishing that he was thinking of me, wanting me by his side instead. I would live every day imagining what my life could have been like if his marriage had only been delayed by a few days.

Mary spoke next to tell Eoin even more news that had yet to be shared. "Yer Aunt Kenna arrived yesterday, Baodan, Eoghanan, and Niall as well. I am unsure of the reason for their visit, but I think 'tis time for ye to go and greet them, let them know that ye are back."

Eoin stood and nodded. "Aye, o'course. I suspect they've come to pay their condolences about Father. They were in the midst of their own grief when he died. I should have reached out to them meself."

"I'll let you visit with them a moment. I'll come up shortly. I want a chance to visit with Blaire. Alone." Bri looked at both her mother and Mary. Understanding, they stood and followed Eoin out of the kitchen.

I stood and moved to the seat across from Bri and silently looked down at the table as I waited for her to speak.

"I'm so sorry. I'm so very, very sorry, Blaire. When we left, there was not the least bit of talk that Arran and Edana would marry. I scarcely saw the two of them together, and he never flirted with her. I never would've come to get you if I'd known."

I wasna angry with her. Of course she wouldna have known, and Eoin certainly wouldna have asked me to return if he'd had any idea. "Ye doona need to apologize to me, Bri. I know that ye dinna know."

"If you want to go back, I'll go once more. I'll help you get set up wherever you like. I can stay with you, teach you some things, get you a good job. I'll even have all of my bank accounts transferred to you, whatever you'd like."

"I doona wanna go back, Bri." I looked up at her as she stood. I got the sudden sense that I wasna going to like whatever it was that she said next.

"I was hoping you would say that. But of course if you hadn't, I really would've helped you go forward again. We're going to go pay Arran a visit. Me and you. We're leaving in the morning."

I shook my head as forcefully as I could, now trying to emulate the frightening eyes I'd thought only earlier I wanted to do my best to avoid. "I will do no such thing. Are ye mad? What good would that bring?"

"I don't know exactly. But I do know that you have to see him. You'll wonder forever if you don't, wonder if he still cares, wonder if you cared for him as much as you thought. If anything, perhaps it will bring you closure."

I'd only known Bri a few weeks, but I could recognize enough of her mother in her to know arguing would not change her mind. "Is this no me decision to make?"

She smiled and shook her head. "No. Not at all. And don't tell Eoin. He'll only try to stop us from leaving. Meet me at the stables at dawn."

She left before I could respond, and I was left to ponder through a sleepless night, just what new humiliation and heartbreak would await me at Arran's new home.

Chapter 18

I was not even given the chance to follow Bri's instructions and meet her down at the stables. Early the next morning with dawn still some time away from peeking through the night's blackness, I heard a knock on the bedchamber door.

Still wide awake, I answered quickly to see Bri with a small bag draped over her shoulders. She couldn't have looked any more excited.

"Come on, let's go! I told Mary of our plan last night so that she could have Kip ready some horses. But don't worry, she promised she wouldn't tell Eoin. I think she's trying to make amends for letting Arran get married."

I shook my head in disagreement. "She has nothing to make amends for. Arran isna a man that is easily kept from doing what he wishes."

Bri's smile briefly disappeared as she stepped into the room to help me gather a few things for the journey. "You're right. I shouldn't have been so harsh on her or my mother. I owe them both an apology. And I'll give them one just as soon as we get back, but right now, we need to go before Eoin rolls over and realizes I've gone."

"Doona ye think he will be furious when he finds out? Do ye no think that he will come after us?"

Bri's smile returned and I found that I was changing my opinion of her. I'd first thought her to be a rather serious-mannered, laced-tight kind of person, but upon spending further time with her,

107

I was learning that she was more mischievous than she let others know. "Well normally I believe yes, he would come after us immediately. But you see, there are guests here now, and I don't think he will leave them. He'll be spit-fire angry I'm sure, but he'll get over it."

"Aye, well he's no me husband. If ye are certain we should go, I willna worry meself over it." I picked up the bag Bri had filled and, moving as silently as we could, we made our way out the back entrance of the castle and to the stables.

A torch burned outside. As we approached, Bri called out to the old stable master, "Kip, are the horses ready?"

"Aye! I already sent Kip back to bed, but they are all ready for us to leave," answered Mary's voice.

Bri and I exchanged a questioning look. "Mary, what are you doing?" We could see inside the stables now. Bri approached Mary to question her. I stood back doing my best to refrain from laughing at the site of the short, round woman balancing astride the horse, beaming with the widest smile I'd ever seen on her.

"What does it look like I'm doing? I'm coming with ye. I've been telling Eoin and Arran for years that I needed a break. After the past few weeks, I feel I've earned it. Besides, I need to see with me own eyes how Arran is faring in his new home." She nudged the horse with her pudgy heels, and it took off at a slow trot out of the stables.

Neither of us argued. After mounting our horses, we followed her. Away from Conall Castle we went.

* * *

It turned out that Bri was perhaps a tad less adventurous than she'd wanted to be. By midday she'd worried herself into such a state of guilt that she rode in complete silence with only her pained expression to keep us company.

I, on the other hand, enjoyed every minute of being astride a horse again. The feeling of being out of the city without the car horns and other modern-day noises that had kept me consistently nervous had me feeling more like myself than I had in ages. As long as I tried to keep our journey's final destination out of my mind, I found myself even feeling happy.

Mary remained cheerful but consistently complained about the torture her backside was experiencing after riding atop a horse for such a long time. My own backside was feeling the effects as well. The months away had softened my previously horse-accustomed bum.

Eventually, as the day progressed, Mary's good humor found a way to crack Bri's worry-creased brow, and the mood lightened. By the time we drew our horses up at the side of a small break in the trees to camp for the evening, all of our middles ached from laughter.

As we dismounted, our bodies stiff and achy, we slowly hobbled along as we made camp, each of us moving as if we were decades older than our given ages. I started a fire while Mary lay out the bread and cheese she'd packed for the journey. Bri went in the direction of a nearby stream to gather some water. Shortly thereafter, we each lay under the stars, our stomachs full and our bodies sore.

I was just on the edge of sleep, and I expected Bri was as well due to the loud snort that burst forth from her. Suddenly, Mary's loud, overly-excited voice caused us to both sit up quite startled.

"What is it, Mary? Did something frighten ye?" I scooted closer to the fire so that I could see the expression on her face more

109

clearly. She looked more excited than anyone should have been after riding for hours and sleeping on the ground.

"Aye, me bum was so sore I almost forgot what I took from Arran's old room. Wake yerselves up, lassies. I have just the thing to soothe our aching bodies."

Bri, who was sitting up but hunched over in a half-asleep position, looked up at Mary from under heavy eyelids. "Sleep? Yes, I believe sleep will do the trick just fine."

"Nay, 'tisna sleep, though I expect we shall all sleep quite soundly after we partake of what I've brought for us. Now wake yerself up." Mary stood and made her way over to her bag propped up against a nearby tree. Reaching inside, she withdrew a large bottle of what was certain to be stronger than wine.

"Mary!" Bri was awake now as her shocked voice echoed through the open space around us, sending the maid into a fit of giggles.

"I told ye that I was in need of a break from me work and a break is what I shall have. I doona think there is anything wrong with Old Mary allowing herself just one night to be foolish. Now, ye lasses will join me whether ye like to or no." She extended two wooden cups in our direction, and we each reached for one without question.

Once they were filled, we all sipped silently, our exhaustion making us far less enjoyable company than Mary seemed to desire. Eventually, I could take no more of Mary's disappointed glares and turned to address Bri.

"Do ye know of any games? I couldna make sense of most of them, but when I was serving drinks in Edinburgh, people would at times play games while they were drinking."

"Well, I'll confess to my lack of drinking knowledge. Teaching gave me little time for a social life, but I suppose I know of one or two games we could play, if Mary still wishes to continue with her wild night."

Mary nodded, smiling wide as she poured more into her cup. "Aye, o'course I do. Have ye yet to see me change me mind about something once it has been set?"

* * *

Shortly thereafter, Bri and I found ourselves tending to a very rambunctious Mary, whom twice had thought it would be a grand idea for us to take off our clothes and run naked through the break in the trees where we'd set up camp.

We'd both quickly done our best to divert her attention elsewhere.

The game "Never Have I Ever" as described by Bri had started off innocently enough. We'd given Mary the opportunity to ask questions first. In her effort to get both of us drunk as well, she'd asked questions that only we could drink to such as, "never have I ever travelled through time." But quickly the questions were turned over to Bri and me. It seemed no matter how wild our statements, Mary had participated in the activity. Soon, I'd learned things about Mary that not only shocked me but made me slightly nervous to be in her company. 'Twas certain neither of us would ever look at the woman quite the same way again.

Thankfully, what seemed to be a never-ending bottle of whiskey finally ran dry. Shortly after, an exhausted and what was sure to be a rather unpleasant Mary come morning, succumbed to sleep.

Chapter 19

Before sunrise, I rose to gather water. The trip hadn't taken me long. While I'd expected to find both Mary and Bri still asleep, I returned to find Mary fully awake, busily ordering Bri to wake up and help her pack up camp. She showed no signs of suffering after her bountiful whiskey consumption, instead seeming rather more rested than both Bri and myself.

"How do ye feel, Mary? I was sure that ye'd sleep for quite a while longer." I bent to roll up my own belongings, following Mary so that we could strap them to our horses.

"I doona know why ye would ask such a question. I feel fine, o'course."

She wouldn't look at me, keeping her head down as we gathered another load to bring back to the horses. Bri joined us this time and, having heard the beginning of our conversation, joined in. "How could you possibly feel fine, Mary? You drank more in the course of an evening than Arran drinks in a day. Do you even remember anything about last night?"

Mary stopped walking and whirled on both of us, quickly setting down her load. "Nay, I doona, and it doesna matter. Both of ye are never to mention what happened last night ever again. Do ye understand? I've never behaved in such a way, and I find meself feeling a wee bit ashamed this morning."

112

I shook my head, interrupting her. "Doona feel that way. There's no need."

Bri nodded. "Yes, please don't feel that way, Mary. You've been under a lot of stress with Eoin and me being gone, Arran leaving, and then the visitors. Not to mention, my mother."

Mary smiled as she seemed to forgive herself just a little. "Aye. We shall blame it on yer mother. Now, let's finish gathering camp and be on our way. I doona wish to spend another night on the ground. I believe that neither of ye will speak of this, no that anyone would believe ye even if ye did."

She was right. No one would. Laughing, we packed up and mounted our horses. It took both Bri and myself to hoist Mary's short legs up on the great beast. As we moved on in the direction of the new Conall Castle, I tried to keep my mind on anything other than the knowledge that I would be seeing Arran again, and meeting his new wife, come nightfall.

* * *

The Castle Formerly Known as Kinnaird

"Did we know that visitors were arriving?" Arran followed the messenger to the entranceway of the castle, all the while wondering if his new guests were just one more thing he'd forgotten. The many duties required by the laird were far more than he'd realized, and each day he found himself being more impressed with the way his brother had handled the responsibilities so soon after their father's death.

"Nay, sir. Ye would have been informed if we had received news of their arrival beforehand. 'Tis three women, sir."

113

Arran stopped before opening the castle's main doors and faced the messenger. "Three women? Do ye know who they are?"

"They say they are from yer old home, sir. An old lady and two women who look like the same person, but they doona talk the same. One of them talks verra strangely."

Arran clasped the man on the shoulder more in an effort to steady himself than to gain the man's attention. It couldn't be true. She was gone, that painful ache in his chest a reminder of her absence every day. "Ye must be mistaken. 'Tis only two women, aye?"

"I'm no mistaken. There are three. The first two insisted I let them in right away, but I told them I wouldna do so until I spoke to ye. The third woman was verra quiet, I noticed her for that reason. See for yerself."

The man pulled the large doors open, giving Arran no time to prepare himself for what he both hoped and dreaded he would find. He found her eyes right away, the pain, passion, and yearning there, a sure reflection of his own.

He wanted to run to her, to gather her in his arms and tell her he was sorry for sending her away, sorry that he hadn't denied his brother and married her when he'd had the chance. He almost did just that, but was stopped by a slight hand on his back.

The touch forced his eyes to jerk away from Blaire involuntarily, and he looked to his side to find Edana.

"I dinna know that Donal had two daughters. They look remarkably similar. Are ye no going to show them inside? They're family, aye?"

"Aye, o'course I am. Would ye go inside and have our table readied for three more? I shall escort them in at once." Edana nodded and turned from him, and he silently chided himself for briefly forgetting the existence of his new wife.

Bri dismounted her horse quickly and came over to him, throwing her arms around his neck and smacking him lightly on the back of his head.

"It's good to see you, but you are a damn fool, Arran. How could you go and do such a stupid, stupid thing?" She whispered it in his ear angrily, and he pulled back to explain, but she quieted him by pulling him in close once again "Don't you dare try to explain it to me right now. We can talk about it after we eat. Go and squeeze Mary, she's been missing you like crazy. And don't say a word to Blaire right now. You can't get her upset before she is forced to sit in front of Edana. You can speak with her later."

She finally loosened her grip, and Arran stepped away. "I doona understand. How is she here? Why?" Questions coursed through his mind, questions that he knew would have to go unanswered for the moment. "What will we tell Edana? She doesna know about the spell room. No one does."

Bri smiled at him reassuringly, but it did nothing to soothe his uneasy mind. "Don't worry, I'll think of something to tell her over dinner. We need to come up with a story anyway. We will have to tell it a lot. No one has seen the both of us together yet. Now, go to Mary and help her down, see her inside. Blaire and I will find our way shortly."

Arran nodded and walked toward Mary whom he quickly helped slide off the back of the horse before yanking her up into a large embrace. He spun her around, kissing her soundly on the cheek before rearing back at the smell that rose around them. "Ye smell like an ale house, Mary. Did ye bathe in a basin of whiskey?"

The old woman flailed in his arms, and her face reddened before she responded to him, smacking him hard on the arm. He seemed to be having that effect on the Conall women this evening. Both Mary and Bri had hit him since their arrival.

"What do ye mean by that? Do ye no know me well enough to believe that I would do such a thing? Why, ye are most likely smelling yerself!"

Arran laughed and stepped away from her. "Aye, I'm sure ye are right, Mary. Now let me show ye inside to yer room where ye shall rest as long as ye are here. Ye work enough at home Mary, I want ye to do naught but breathe."

She laughed, and Arran pulled her in close. Doing his best to avoid Blaire, he looked down while showing Mary inside.

* * *

A knock on the bedchamber door caused my breath to lodge in my throat, but upon hearing Bri's voice on the other side, I breathed a deep sigh of relief. I swung the door open to be greeted with the hefty smell of meat and wine as Bri carried my dinner inside.

"Here you go. It was difficult for me to explain why I needed to bring you food when supposedly you were too ill to go to dinner. I'm sure Arran knew I was lying."

I sat quickly, shoveling the delicious meal into my mouth as it eased me grumbling stomach. "I shouldna have come here. It was wrong of me to do so. Did ye no see the way Edana looked at him when she came outside?"

Bri crossed her arms as she stared down at me. "No. I didn't. I was too busy looking at how Arran couldn't take his eyes off you."

116

"He dinna even speak to me." I quickly finished off the food and stood, moving to the door. "I canna stay here, Bri. I'm going back tonight."

I made to open the door but was stopped by Bri's tight grip on my arm. "Ok, if you want to go, that's fine. We will leave tomorrow, but you can't go anywhere tonight. You don't know the way back by yourself anyhow. I'm sorry. It was wrong of me to make you come here."

I could see the sense in her words. It would be foolish for me to travel at night all alone, but I knew that I couldna spend another moment inside the castle. "Doona be sorry. Ye have no reason to be so. Ye are right. I willna leave, but I need to get outside of the castle. I dinna know seeing him would upset me so. I'll be in the stables, brushing the horses."

I shut the door before Bri had a chance to speak.

Chapter 20

Arran knocked lightly on the door, hoping that Bri would open it quickly before Edana saw him sneaking into the room of their female guests. She'd been away in her own bedchamber for some time, but he knew her to be a nighttime wanderer. She was finding her way into his own bed much more frequently.

Blaire's absence at dinner had surprised him. He knew she wasn't ill, not that he could blame her for not wanting to see him. She must think he truly didn't care for her, to be able to marry so soon after what they had shared together. If only Blaire knew how she occupied his every thought, pained his every breath when he wasn't near her.

"Come in. Did you not hear me calling you through the door telling you that you could enter?"

He'd lost himself in his own thoughts of regret and self-pity, forgetting that he was standing outside the door until he heard Bri's voice in front of him. He looked up, pulling himself out of his trance as he stepped inside. "Nay, I dinna. I was thinking."

"I'm sure you were. What did you think about what I told Edana about me and Blaire? Do you think she bought it? Will everybody else?"

Arran frowned as he tried to remember what story Bri had told. It was the last thing on his mind, all he could think about was

Blaire. "Forgive me, I doona know what ye told her. I am no feeling like meself."

Bri reached out to lay a hand on his back and he smiled, knowing she understood.

"I know. I'm sorry. We can talk about it later. She's not here, Arran. She said she was going to the stables."

He nodded, briefly shutting his eyes as he pictured her there, slender fingers running gently down whatever horse was lucky enough to share her company. "O'course she is. The lass loves horses as much as I do. She willna want to see me though. Why is she here, Bri? How did she get back to this time?"

"Eoin and I went for her. That's where we were, not at Bran's."

Arran had suspected as much. Not that they'd traveled into the future, but he knew they weren't at Bran's. They would have learned about his wedding much sooner if they'd only gone as far as the village. "Why did ye do so?"

"Because I could see that you were miserable, and I believed that Blaire was still in love with you as well."

"And is she?" Arran turned away from her, his heart nearly stopping at the anticipation he felt at his question. It was wrong of him to ask, to care, he'd promised himself to another, but Blaire had claimed ownership of his heart long before he ever knew of Edana Kinnaird.

"Of course she is. She would never have dreamed of coming back here if she wasn't. We didn't know you were going to run off and get married. You don't love her, do you? Edana?"

"I'll no speak poorly of Edana, but I'll no lie to ye either and tell ye that I love her. It matters not. I am married to the lass, and there is nothing that can be done to change it." The truth of his own

119

words hit him square in the chest, and he found himself leaning a hand against the wall to keep himself from doubling over. "Ye know the truth of me words as well. Why did ye bring her here if ye knew I couldna be with her?"

"Because things didn't end properly between the two of you. Now she needs closure, to know that it is finished between the two of you and that you have both said your peace. And you need it too."

He inhaled deeply, trying to catch the breath that seemed lodged in between his ribs. "I shall go to Blaire. I must speak with her and see her once more before I lose her again. I've spent every moment since she left believing that I would never see her again. Now that she is back, I canna deny meself what I've been yearning for every moment. I know we canna be together, but I must see that she is well and apologize for the hurt me foolishness has caused her."

"Yes, go, but end it, Arran. Don't allow either of you to walk away, hoping for something that can no longer be. It would only make it harder for both of you."

He nodded, turning away from Bri as he silently opened the bedchamber door to make his leave.

* * *

The ground behind me crunched, the coldness in the air hardening all of nature. The noise was a sure sign someone was approaching. Part of me hoped it would be him, but part of me hoped that the footsteps behind me were a figment of my mind. I was furious, hurt, and humiliated by my presence here. It was wrong of me to have come here, to be in the place he shared with

120

his new wife, but I wanted to see him, to hold him, to know that it wasna only me that was pained by our last moments spent together before I traveled forward in time.

"Bri told me I would find ye here. I dinna think I would ever see ye again, Blaire."

My hand froze as it moved down the side of the chestnut colored mare. "Aye, I suppose ye dinna."

"I'm pleased to see ye. It has been verra hard for me since ye went away."

He was lying I was certain, words meant to make me weak in front of him and cause me to confess my true feelings. I'd done so once before, only to be sent away heartbroken. I wouldna allow myself to be so foolish again. "Oh, has it? I dinna believe ye were that fond of me."

He grabbed me by the arm, pulling me away from the mare as he spun me so that I faced him. I was close to him, our chests nearly touching, as he stared down at me angrily. "Doona do that, Blaire. I came here to apologize to ye, but I willna allow ye to behave as if ye believe that I dinna care for ye. Look into me eyes and tell me if ye believe that I doona still."

I couldna breathe. His grip on me was tight, and all I could see were his eyes, pained and hungry. My own chest started to rise and fall rapidly, and I yanked away from him. "Ye doona need to apologize for no wanting me. Ye canna help who ye love. I hope that ye and Edana will be verra happy together." I walked as quickly as I could away from him, desperate to get back to the safety of the castle. We were too alone here, and if he touched me again, I was afraid I wouldna be able to push myself away once more.

121

He was too quick. This time he dinna only grab my arm but gripped me tightly by both wrists as he pulled me back into the confined shelter of the stables. Once inside, he leaned against the door of an empty stable as he pulled me against him, my wrists and front flush against his chest. I kept my hands in fists, unwilling to allow them to lay against him, certain I would uncoil at the touch of my hands on him once more.

He was tense as if suppressing something deep within him. He dinna speak, dinna move, only held me there close to him as we stared silently at one another. Slowly, our breathing quickened, our chests matching the rise and fall of each other's. His eyes dropped to my lips, only to dart upward once more.

I could feel danger approaching, feelings unsaid threatening to express themselves through touch, and I squirmed within his grasp hoping that I could move away and break the tension surrounding us.

He dinna allow it and only pulled me closer, leaning forward to plead breathlessly in my ear. "Doona move, lass." He pulled his head back so that his eyes pierced my own. "I know...I know I canna have ye, but ye were right. I canna help who I love and, married or no, I love ye, Blaire. I should never have sent ye away. To be separated from ye these past months has been hell. Ye have to know that I dinna mean a word I said then. If I were a better man, I would never have done what I did to ye. If I were a better man, I wouldna do this to ye now."

His lips, trembling and warm, pressed against my own. I melted, allowing the man I'd yearned so long for to hold me in his arms as I'd dreamed of him doing for what seemed like ages.

I should've pulled away and run back to the safety of the castle. Around such company, he would never have been so bold, but here, with no one to serve as witness to our actions but our consciences, he held me tightly against him, his eyes and mouth hungry, his body trembling as he struggled with his conflicting emotions.

He wanted me badly, and my own heart was beating such that I could scarcely think beyond the next touch of his lips. But Arran was a good man, and I could feel his struggle in the tension in his arms, hard muscles holding him back from surrender, back from the act that would sever his sacred marriage vows. Despite his past philandering ways, it was not in him to decide such a thing. It was not in me to ask this of him.

He restrained. His lips were eager, yet reserved. His body was tight as a bow string as he waited for me to either send him away or invite him into my arms. The decision was mine, and in that instant I could see the future that lay ahead of me, one of solitude. Arran and I couldna be together in the way we both desired, as husband and wife. But our love needed to be validated, to be expressed in such a way that we could both hold on to the memory that our hearts belonged to one another even as we made our way through life apart. I couldna deny myself one night of the presence of his love.

"Arran," I whispered his name softly, opening my fists so that the palms of my hands rested against his chest. It was enough to make him pull away and await my decision. His eyes were red and heavy, glassy and moist with unshed tears. He lifted his head away but kept a tight grip on my wrists, silently pleading with me to give him the permission both of us yearned for.

"Aye, lass?" His voice was dry and cracked as the words struggled to find their way out of him.

123

"I know the truth of what yer marriage means for us, but I doona have the strength to walk away from ye this night. Please Arran, tonight allow me to love ye."

He crushed his mouth to mine, his arms moving around me as he released my wrists and pulled me hard against him. I moved my hands up to the sides of his face, running my fingers through his hair as I heard him swallow a hard lump in the back of his throat.

I rubbed my thumb gently across his cheek, pausing as I touched a droplet of wetness that quickly found its way onto my tongue, its salty bite bringing tears to my own eyes. I'd known him all of my life, and I'd never seen him cry.

I pulled my lips away from his, moving upward as I kissed the tiny corner on the inside of his eye from which the tear had fallen. He pulled away, rubbing his hands quickly over his face as he smiled, embarrassed that his tear has been seen. "I'm sorry, lass. What a fool I must look to ye."

I cupped either side of his face and kissed him gently. "Ye are no a fool. Ye are the man I love, and if I shall burn in hell for it, I shall have ye this night. If ye shall have me as well?"

I felt him smile against my mouth as his whispered, warm breath tickled my cheek. "Aye, I shall have ye, lass. Over and over again, tonight ye shall be mine alone." He paused in between words, roaming his lips over my face as he kissed my brows, my cheekbones, my chin. "I have been a frozen shell since ye left, Blaire. Tis only in this moment as I feel the warmth of yer skin beneath me mouth that I feel me heart begin to thaw. Now, let me kiss the rest of ye, every bit, so that yer warmth and light may finally melt away me frigid coat and make me whole again."

His fingers moved to my laces, and as I shut my eyes reveling in the feeling of his fingertips against my skin, I felt my dress fall away. I'd never stood naked in front of a man but, rather than fear, warmth rushed over me as I watched his hungry eyes roam, filled with adoration and love at my bare body.

"God, Blaire. Ye canna know how beautiful ye are."

He pushed open the stall door behind him, and I moved past him into the empty stable. There was no hay, and the stable was freshly swept as I stood nervously, my back toward him as I waited for him to proceed. I could hear him shedding his kilt, and before I had a chance to face him, he pressed himself against me. His chest pushed against my back as he brought his hands around to cup my breasts. I moaned as he caressed my nipples, his lips planting moist kisses down the curve of my neck.

I turned into him, reaching for his head so that I could pull him down toward me. Our lips met with a heated passion, no longer restrained from our previous hesitation. The decision was made, and now we came together quickly, taking no time to explore each other's bodies. That could come later in the night. Now, with the knowledge that we could no always be together in this way, desperation filled us. We could no bear to be apart from one another a moment more.

Our lips danced in a painful frenzy. When neither of us could stand it a moment more, Arran bent his knees, pulling me down with him so that we lay on the stable floor. I opened myself to him, only nodding as he thrust himself deep inside me. With nothing to ready me, I screamed loudly before he muffled my cry with his mouth.

The pain diminished quickly and, as we found our rhythm, the night faded away and any thought of tomorrow or yesterday was as distant as the time in the future that had separated us from each other for far too long.

Chapter 21

Arran, the fool, thought he and his whore had gone unseen, of that Tormod was certain. But the two lovers had moaned such throughout the night that even the horses in the stables had been kept awake. Tormod had kept a tight watch on the castle, waiting for anything he could use against the man who had stolen his right to be laird.

Finally, his waiting had paid off. He'd long heard of Arran Conall's philandering ways, and a man accustomed to such varied bedfellows was unlikely to change his habits after marriage. A better partner Tormod couldn't have dreamed up himself. For it wasn't just any lustful whore that Arran had bedded. Arran had made his way into the stables with his brother's wife.

It was a grand opportunity, one if which played properly, he knew he could use to destroy both Conall brothers. Edana already hated them, but once he shared what he'd seen last night, he knew she'd be willing to do even what he was about to ask of her.

He waited inside the home he shared with his sister, watching for any sign of his pale-haired and plain-faced pawn to make her way through the village. She met him there each morning while Arran went on his daily ride. Their moments together were short, but each moment he was forced to spend in her company, talking, kissing, tupping, made him hate her all the more.

What a pathetic creature, so willingly giving him her trust at the first sign of his forced affection. She was ignorant, stupid, and Tormod found nothing less attractive in a woman.

"I see her coming. I shall be away now."

"Wait." Tormod called out for his sister to stop before she made her way out of the door. "Do ye think 'tis wise to ask her to do what ye suggested? If she isna pregnant, Arran will surely know before too long."

Tormod flinched at the look Fia threw in his direction. "Aye, Arran will feel guilt over his betrayal of Edana, but 'tis no her place to forbid him from doing so. If she tells him she's carrying his child, his remorse will multiply on its own, making him weak, just as we need him to be. She is coming. Make love to yer fool."

Once his sister left, Tormod moved to the doorway looking each direction to ensure that none would see her enter his home. It was unlikely he knew. People kept away from them. His sister's company was a pleasure most did not seek, for she was a woman of strength, not a woman of pity like the wretch that now made her way inside.

"Tormod."

He stiffened as Edana threw her arms around him. He pulled away from her as he motioned for her to sit next to him. "I have something to tell ye, Edana, something we can finally use against Arran."

"Aye, are ye going to tell me that Arran has been with someone else? I know he dinna stay in his room."

Tormod's brows lifted in surprise, perhaps the lass was visiting her husband's bed more often than he'd realized. It was all the better. It would make their tale all the more believable. "Aye, he has, but no just with anyone. He spent the night with his brother's wife."

Edana shook her head, and Tormod lifted his brows even further. He'd been certain it was Eoin's wife he'd seen with Arran.

"Nay, 'twas no Bri, 'twas was the other one, the one he couldna keep his eyes off of when they arrived. It seems that Donal MacChristy is more interesting than most people believed. I always thought that Bri was just how people close to them referred to Blaire, but ye see, Blaire is a different daughter entirely. Donal had two daughters, twins, and he sent one of them to grow up with his brother."

"Ye canna mean it? How could no one know of this?" His brows were about to lift off his head, and Tormod did his best to straighten his face into some semblance of normalcy. This was the most interested he'd ever been in Edana's words.

"They said that Donal was afraid he couldna care for both girls after their mother died. He sent Bri away, and she spent most of her life traveling in the care of her uncle, which goes a far way toward explaining the odd way which she speaks. Blaire stayed here, and it was she that was supposed to marry Eoin. But before the wedding, Bri returned home, and it was she that Eoin fell in love with, no Blaire. But it seems that Arran has stepped in where his brother has failed."

"I've never seen two lasses so similar in appearance." Tormod leaned back and shook his head in surprise.

"Aye, 'tis quite remarkable. But it was most certainly she that ye saw with Arran, no Bri. I saw Bri after I noticed that Arran was no in his room."

"Aye, I suppose it must have been. Regardless, I know what we must do to weaken Arran." He leaned forward and grabbed

Edana's hands, knowing the effect his touch had on her. She yearned for him, and any touch he was willing to give her would only make her more amenable to his plan.

"What is it?" She stood from her chair and moved to his lap. Tormod had to keep himself from grimacing as their bodies touched.

"Ye have been sharing his bed, aye?" He shifted trying to scoot her away from him, but she only leaned in closer, squirming her bottom in his lap such that his manhood nearly betrayed his disgust with her.

"Aye, but each time 'tis only ye that I see in my mind. Arran is only the vessel I use to reach ye when we are apart." She kissed him then, and part of him lifted, causing him to swiftly stand so that Edana would not take notice. If she did, it would mean he would have to tup her now, and he'd be forced to hold her in his arms until she left. 'Twas best to wait until a few short moments before their time together ended so that he could give her just enough to keep her believing in the fallacy of his love and painless enough for himself that it was bearable.

"Aye, well good. He should believe ye then when ye tell him that ye are with child. I shall find a nurse to confirm yer story."

"Why? I am no with child, and it wouldna take too long before Arran would notice that I was not." The pitch of her voice was high and painful to Tormod's ears. He turned away from her to grimace at the wall.

"By the time Arran would notice, ye may very well actually be with child, whether it be mine or his. And any remorse that Arran feels for having slept with another will only cause him more pain if he believes ye are carrying his child. His love for his unborn child and his guilt over betraying ye will make him weak." He could sense that she was about to contest. Rather than listen to the sound of her voice once again, he crushed himself to her and sat about his daily task of making his fool love him.

*   *   *

Conall Castle

"Slow down, Adelle. I canna understand ye when ye speak so quickly."

Adelle threw her hands up in exasperation as she stood before Eoin, who was decidedly too calm over their present situation. It was clear he hadn't heard her, or she was certain he would be much more panicked than he was.

"Donal MacChristy is here. Jeepers, I've never seen a man so closely resemble my ex-husband. I nearly jumped out of my skin when I saw him. He came to see Blaire. He said he wants to see his daughter! I didn't know what to tell him so I just had Kip take him to the stables so that they could get his horse situated." Adelle watched as her words sunk in, and Eoin's formerly calm face began to match her own.

"Christ, o'course he would show up whilst Bri is away. She canna even pretend to be Blaire if she isna here. How will I explain to him that his daughter went to visit me brother without me? He will hardly think it proper. And it isna! That's why she left without me. She knew I wouldna have let her go."

Adelle cleared her throat to interrupt him. "That isn't our only problem. When they do get back, how are we going to explain to him that there are two Blaires?"

131

Chapter 22

The Castle Formerly Known as Kinnaird

Morning came much too quickly, and with it the sadness that had been momentarily lifted slowly seeped back into my heart. As light started to peek through the small cracks in the stable doors, I felt Arran shift beside me, and I turned my head so that I could kiss his brow.

The tilt of my head sent a tear that sat dormant in the corner of my eye running down my face, and I quickly reached up to brush it away.

I'd no slept a wink through the night, and after our lovemaking ended, Arran drifted away into the slumber of a man who'd no slept soundly in quite a long time. He'd held me tightly, squeezing his arms around me if I shifted only a little, as if he was afraid I would get up and leave him during the night.

Perhaps I should have, but my heart was torn into two very distinct pieces, and the confusion of feelings left me frozen and as trapped in the stables as Arran's heavy arms. I had never felt such love, such joy, never known just how deeply two souls could connect through touch. I had also never been so heartbroken. The sadness I felt at knowing this was the only time we would be together caused me to ache all the way down to my bones.

"I doona wish to move from this place, lass. Do ye think we could hide away here and live with the horses?"

132

I smiled and kissed him lightly before forcing myself to stand and dress. "Nay, as much as I wish it, we canna. If I doona return before Mary awakes, ye know she shall have all those in the castle looking for us."

"That she will, lass."

He stood, doing nothing to hide what morning had done to him, and my face reddened at the sight of him. "How will I get back into the castle unseen?"

"I doona expect that anyone will question ye. If they do, just tell them ye went out for a morning walk. I shall leave from here to go out on me daily ride. I shall see ye all before ye return home." He gathered me up in his arms, pulling me in close so that I could scarcely breathe. "I love ye, lass, and I doona believe that I can say goodbye to ye. When I can, I shall come to ye. From now on, me marriage to Edana will be only for her protection, but my heart shall always belong to ye. In time, Edana will learn to accept it."

I tensed and pulled away from him. I couldna have him make promises to me that I knew couldna be. Arran was a good man, and shortly he would feel remorse for our actions. Once he did, he would no come to me again. "'Tis best for ye to no leave me with hope when it isna there."

He grabbed me quickly, silencing me with his mouth as he caused my head to spin and my knees to buckle. "I willna let ye go, Blaire. I canna do so again. Tell me that if I come for ye that ye will see me. I must live with the hope of holding ye in me arms once more."

The tears fell freely now. Any resistance I had shattered. If he came to me, I would welcome him. I was no strong enough to deny him. All that I was had been his for quite some time already. "Aye,

I will. Now, leave. Bri and Mary will be awake soon. I should make me way back inside."

"I love ye, Blaire. When ye left this time, ye took me heart with ye, and it has belonged to no one else."

He kissed me once more, dressed, and moved to open the stable doors so that he could mount his horse and depart on his ride. He smiled as he left. Once he was gone, I scanned the horizon. Seeing it clear, I made my way back to the castle.

* * *

Bri was awake when I arrived back at the room. 'Twas apparent she'd been so for quite a while.

"Oh Blaire, I'm glad you're back. I couldn't sleep a wink after Arran came by here looking for you. Are you okay?"

She stood from where she was seated on the edge of the bed and pulled me into a quick embrace.

"Aye, I shall be, in time. We should make our leave today."

She was kind enough not to question me further and left to wake Mary.

Once Bri had left the room, I cleaned myself using the small basin of water that sat at the back of the room. After changing, I did my best to pin my hair so that it dinna look like I spent the night in the stables.

I struggled with an unruly hair that was difficult to reach at the nape of my neck. It stuck out in a way that defied gravity, but unable to see it, I found myself useless when it came to securing it into place.

Thankfully, Bri re-entered the room and seeing my difficulty, came to offer her assistance. As she grabbed the long piece of hair, combing through it with her fingers, I asked her about Mary.

"Was she still sleeping when ye went to wake her?" While Bri worked on the back, I kept my hands busy trying to soothe the frizzing strands around my forehead.

"She was awake, but lounging in a steamy tub with three ladies sitting around her waiting on her hand and foot. Arran wasn't joking when he said she wasn't to lift a finger while she's here."

I laughed, picturing Mary ordering the poor lasses about. I was certain she would be no too pleased with having to leave Arran so soon. "What did she say to ye when ye told her we were leaving?"

Bri chuckled, and I caught her eyes roll in the small mirror before us. "Nothing that I wish to repeat. She said that we were welcome to leave if we wish, but she was making this her permanent home because Arran was the only one to show her any appreciation in ages. But don't worry, she'll come. In fact, I expect she will be ready for departure before us. Whether she will admit it or not, it's driving her crazy not to be ruling over her roost. There. Does that feel better?"

I reached behind and smiled as the piece was no longer floating toward the ceiling and nodded in approval. "Aye, thank ye."

A knock at the door and Mary's boisterous voice from behind it signaled that Bri was right. Soon we would take our leave from the castle, from Arran, and from the place my heart would always remain.

* * *

Edana stood back after saying her own polite and expected farewells, watching closely as Arran made his own. He'd given her no explanation, made no excuse for his absence from his bedchamber the night before. Perhaps he thought she'd not come for him and believed his absence had gone unnoticed.

Even before Tormod's words, Edana had taken notice of her husband's empty bedchamber, and she'd suspected that he'd spent his night with another. She couldna say she was surprised. The wandering ways of Arran Conall had been legendary as she was growing up, and she didn't know a single lass who didn't dream of sharing her bed with him. But this knowledge did nothing to slow the torment of anger that spread its fiery touch over her each time she pictured them together. It didn't matter that she was in love with another as well. Arran was a fool. 'Twas only right that she should find a true man elsewhere, but she should have been enough for Arran.

At first, she'd been resistant to Tormod's suggestion that she lie to Arran about a pregnancy, but as she watched him lean into Blaire as he pulled her close, unable to stop his lips from lingering near her cheek and the undeniable yearning that shown in his eyes, she realized the awful truth. Arran had not only shared his bed with the whore, but his heart as well. Whatever loyalty Arran had once felt for her, it had diminished overnight. In order to keep him close, malleable to her plans, she had to regain his loyalty.

She would do as Tormod bid, and by sundown she would win back Arran's heart by becoming pregnant with her non-existent child.

Chapter 23

The first day of our journey back to Conall Castle was a pensive one. I remained wrapped in my own thoughts of loss and guilt. Although 'twas no I married to Edana, I couldna deny the guilt I felt over her. She was an innocent victim of our love for one another, albeit an unpleasant one. I'd only spent a few moments with her, but I was certain a friendship would never have been possible between us under any circumstance.

She was entirely miserable looking, and something about her made me uneasy, as if she knew what had occurred between Arran and me. I was sure that we'd gone unseen the night before out in the stables, but the glare Edana shot in my direction as we departed made me question whether or not we were as alone as we'd believed.

The second day of our journey, the day we were due to arrive back at the castle, proved to be more eventful.

Mary complained regularly about us ending her rare treat of luxury so soon, but it was easy to see the jest in her words. With each hoof step that brought us closer to Conall Castle, Mary's smile grew. I could tell she was itching to resume her duties as the true leader of the castle.

After what was at least her dozenth time complaining, she suddenly changed the subject and addressed me so bluntly that I nearly fell off my horse in surprise. "Ye slept with him, dinna ye?"

"Mary!" Bri's shocked and elevated voice echoed through the countryside.

"What? Ye have been thinking the same thing, have ye no? I saw the way Arran looked at her and she at him when we left. 'Twas no a look that people share unless they are intimately acquainted." Mary gave Bri an expression that dared her to disagree.

"I may have been thinking it, but I have the tact not to say it or ask her. Goodness, Mary, I swear you get more nosy with each passing day."

"I'm no nearly nosy enough!"

"Aye, we did. But I doona wish to discuss it further," I interrupted, knowing that it was best to give Mary the information she desired rather than have it forced from me by the persistence of her words.

"I knew it, but doona ye worry, lass. I'll no be judging ye for it. Arran's marriage is no one built on love, and it never should have happened."

Sympathy was evident in her eyes, and it only increased the longing for him deep within my chest.

We were nearing the castle when a rider off in the distance caused Bri to groan aloud as she slowed the pace of her horse.

"Crap, it's Eoin. He's not going to be excited to see me. I bet he's so angry, he's ready to lock me away."

She laughed, but it was an uncomfortable one. I could tell she was nervous for his reaction.

"Doona worry. He may be angry, but I've known the lad all his life. He knows by now that ye canna control women. He will just be glad that ye've returned. Besides, it looks as if he is riding

138

for us. He must have news he hoped would reach us before we arrive back home."

Mary's revelation caused us all to slow the pace of our horses as we waited in anticipation for Eoin.

He rode quickly and reined to a halt beside us. "Ach! There ye are ye three naughty lassies. Why, I should throw the three of ye in the dungeon where ye canna cause any more trouble." He smiled, showing his jest. "But first, I want to kiss me wife. Come here, ye awful scoundrel." Eoin maneuvered his horse so that it was next to Bri's and deftly lifted her off her own horse so that she straddled him on his. He smacked her behind softly and proceeded to kiss her as Mary and I watched awkwardly.

Eventually Mary interrupted. "All right, that's enough! Stop it, the both of ye. I was feeling quite hungry and ready for a meal once we arrive back at the castle, but I think ye've spoiled me appetite."

"Oh hush, Mary. There's some remaining for ye as well." Eoin dismounted, pulling Bri down from the horse with him. Once they were both on the ground, he moved to Mary's side, reaching for her as he pulled her off the horse and into a tight embrace. He kissed her soundly on the cheek. She squealed and protested in his arms, but her red cheeks and wide smile showed her joy at reuniting with one of her boys.

"'Tis good to see ye as well, Blaire. I'm glad that ye have all arrived back safely, although ye should never have gone alone." Eoin sat Mary on the ground and stepped away to regard all of us. "Ye left Adelle and me with quite a mess to trouble ourselves over. Not only our guests, but yer father arrived last night as well."

"Me father?" My voice croaked as I said the words, and I made to dismount my own horse as I was afraid that I might faint right off the top of it if I dinna. As far as I knew, my father believed that it was I married to Eoin. He had no idea that I had spent the last months in a different century. He would have to be told the truth. Whether or no he would be able to believe it, I knew not.

"Aye, his arrival was unexpected. He said he was eager to see his daughter. I've done what I could to distract him, but he is verra disgruntled and losing patience. 'Tis best that we get all of ye back as quickly as possible so that the two of ye," he pointed to Bri and myself, "can give him whatever explanation ye choose."

"So ye told him nothing?" Part of me hoped Eoin would have explained everything to him, but it seemed that he'd left that unpleasant task undone. No that I could blame him.

"Nay. I told him that ye'd accompanied Mary into the village to gather some supplies for the castle, and he was no too pleased to hear it. He thought it unwise of me to allow ye to go alone. I canna imagine what he would think of me if he learned I'd allowed ye to travel as far off as ye did."

Eoin ran his hand over his face, clearly exhausted after dealing with my father. I'd yet to see him, and fatigue was already overcoming me at the prospect.

He was a good man, and I loved him, but my independent spirit had made me a difficult child to manage. He'd been pleased when he'd finally been able to marry me off into the hands of another to oversee my behavior. He would no be pleased to know that his efforts had been unsuccessful. I was afraid he would feel it meant that he had ownership over me once more. If so, he would be disappointed. I would no be going back home with him, even if I had to work with Mary in the Conall's kitchens. I re-mounted my horse and gestured to Eoin, Bri, and Mary to do the same.

"Let's be on with it then. I doona wish to keep him waiting."

* * *

"I canna believe it, truly. If ye dinna both stand before me now, I would never be able to believe such a story. I always knew Morna was a witch, but I never believed she would be capable of such a grand spell. Why, ye've given an old man the shock of his life."

My father laughed deeply as he squeezed me around my middle as I sat upon his lap. His reaction to our story was astonishing. Rather than doubt or anger, he'd accepted our explanation with pure curiosity.

"So ye are no angry with me? And ye will go along with what we told Edana, claiming us both as yer daughters?" I returned his squeeze, no longer nervous at his being here, but simply enjoying the feeling of safety that came with being wrapped in my father's arms.

"Nay, I'm no angry. I doona see how either of ye had a choice in what happened. And aye, I shall be pleased to call Bri as me own. I've thought she was for some time now." He smiled in Bri's direction. "Ye did a remarkable job of fooling me. Ye are a magnificent trickster."

Bri laughed and shook her head in disagreement. "With all due respect, I believe your bad ear went a long way to making my performance believable to you."

"Ach, I'm sure ye are right, lass." Father reached up and touched his left ear that lacked any ability to hear.

Bri stood from her seat in the spell room and moved to give us some privacy. We'd met him down there hoping that the presence of Morna's spell books would help him to believe.

141

"I'll leave the two of you to visit alone for awhile. You know, I think it's fitting that I should be known as your daughter. You bear a striking resemblance to my real father."

She winked at both of us. Once she was gone, my father stood and grabbed my hand so that he could lead me out of the spell room.

"Let's go for a walk down by the sea, shall we? I'm anxious to hear of me bonny lass' adventures while she was away."

I nodded, and together we left hand-in-hand. In that moment, I felt closer to my father than I'd ever felt before.

Chapter 24

The Castle Formerly Known as Kinnaird

"Ye have been drinking less as of late, have ye no?"

Her voice startled him. Arran turned away from the window he'd been staring out of, imagining where Blaire was, what she was doing, and if she was thinking of him as well. One week had passed since Blaire had returned to Conall Castle. Although she was days away, his world seemed brighter just knowing he could get to her, and she was no longer out of his reach in another century.

Every night since their departure, Edana had come to him, softly knocking on his door in the middle of the night. He'd ignored it, never giving explanation, hoping that within time she would give up and cease seeking his affection.

Tonight was the only night she'd entered his room uninvited. He faced her, doing his best to feign a smile. Over the past days, he'd come to learn more about his new wife, and what he'd seen from her had made it even easier for him to push aside any guilt he might have felt over his feelings for Blaire.

He'd watched as she screamed and ordered servants about as if they were criminals rather than the loyal and hardworking members of their household that they were. 'Twas a habit she'd learned from her father no doubt, but a needless act of malevolence nonetheless.

143

Her moods shifted suddenly. It was impossible for him to tell when he was seeing glimpses of her true self. He hoped it was her moments of kindness, but something warned him that her moments of ill-tempered outbursts ran deep into her core.

With each day, he grew more certain that she was not a shy, helpless victim, not a beaten woman who needed his aid as he once believed. If only he'd not been so foolish, rushing into a commitment when he knew not to whom he was committing. He could be welcoming the woman he loved into his bed rather than denying his wife entry into it.

"Aye, ale is no so appealing to me as it once was. Why are ye awake so late in the evening, Edana?"

"I needed to speak to me husband. Have ye no heard me knocking on yer door these past nights? Have ye already seen what it is I'm here to tell ye, and ye no longer find me so pleasing?"

He didn't know what she was talking about. He'd noticed nothing from her, hardly seeing her when he looked right at her, so occupied his mind was with thoughts of Blaire. "Aye, lass, I heard ye, but I have been tired. I have no been in the mood for company in bed. But nay, I have no noticed anything about ye. What do ye mean by that?"

"I'm with child, Arran."

Shock coursed painfully through him, and he found that he was gripping the edge of the table so tightly that his knuckles shown white beneath his skin. "Nay, lass. We have no been married long enough for ye to be carrying a child. Even if ye were, it would be too soon for ye to know it." He hoped that he was right, but he knew little of such things, and he knew that his words came more from wishful thinking than true knowledge.

"Aye, 'tis true that we have no been married long, but 'tis still verra possible for it to be so. I have no bled, and I have never no done so before. Me nurse has confirmed it as well."

Arran pulled the stool out from the small desk and plopped himself down on it, his head suddenly heavy and throbbing.

Edana motioned to someone standing in the doorway. Shortly after, a woman who looked to be about Mary's age approached him. She was short and slight. There were dark circles beneath her eyes. He thought she looked too unhealthy herself to be nurse to anyone but still rose to greet her. Before he could speak, Edana interrupted.

"Go on, tell him. Tell him what ye just told me, that I am carrying his bairn."

Edana's tone caused him to look attentively toward the nurse who stood before him. There seemed to be an underlying threat with Edana's words, and the look of fear on the poor woman's face was enough for him to be sure he was right.

"May I speak to yer nurse alone for a moment, Edana?" He expected her response and fumbled quickly for an answer that would placate her.

"Do ye no believe me? What reason would I have to lie?"

"Nay, lass, I believe ye. If ye say ye are with child, I believe that ye are. 'Tis only I have a private matter of a personal nature I would like to have seen." He smiled politely at the nurse.

Edana rolled her eyes as she slowly made her way toward the door. "Fine. Suit yerself, but ye know that she is no a real doctor. She deals only with birthing and such matters. If something troubles ye, ye should see the man in the village."

"'Tis only a small matter. I suppose any woman with knowledge of herbs could help me with this. Go on. I shall come to ye shortly, and we shall talk."

With Edana gone, Arran motioned for the nurse to sit on the stool in front of his desk. "What is yer name, miss?"

The woman's voice was quiet and shaky. It pained Arran to know that she must have been mistreated by the people of this castle for some time to be so frightened in his presence before she even knew him.

"My name is Gara, and I'm afraid that she is right, sir. I doona know much of healing and only a little of herbs. Perhaps ye should seek help elsewhere. I wouldna want to mislead ye."

Arran crouched down in front of Gara, smiling to ease the woman's nerves. "Doona worry, lass. All is well with me. I only wanted to speak to ye without Edana being present. Now I wish that ye tell me the truth. Do ye know Edana to be with child?"

"Aye, sir."

"Ye doona have to worry, lass. If she's threatened ye, all ye need to do is tell me so. I'll believe ye, and I will ensure yer protection. Has she done so?"

Surprise flickered in the woman's eyes, and Arran allowed himself to hope that perhaps Edana's words had been a lie.

"Nay, sir. She is carrying yer child as ye shall see soon enough. Now, may I be excused from ye, sir?"

Arran stood so that the woman could move from her seat and extended his arm out beside him. "Aye, lass. Ye are no being held against yer will. Thank ye for speaking to me and for yer honesty."

"'Tis my pleasure to be of service to ye, sir."

Gara stood and nodded before turning away from him, but Arran called out to her once more before she could leave the room.

"I know that things have no always been good for the people of this castle and while I claim no responsibility for yer suffering, I am sorry for it. I vow that I will do all that I can to change things from now on. Doona ever be afraid in me presence."

"Thank ye, sir."

She slipped out quickly leaving Arran alone to think about the unborn child that was seemingly on its way to him.

* * *

Gara hurried down the hallway, breathing in deeply and swiftly wiping at her face to hide the tears.

Arran Conall was a fine man. He would be a good laird to her and to her people. It did not sit well with her to lie to him, but she needed the payment for her family. The death of her husband had placed a burden on her that she'd been unable to adequately meet for some time. This lie would guarantee her family a roof over their heads for a long while. She was willing to put aside her morals for the sake of her children at home.

Still, it was not right, and she'd live with the guilt over such an injustice for all of her years to come. With each passing day, she would search for a way to make amends.

Chapter 25

"Did she do it, Tormod?"

He walked through the doorway of his home, not surprised to find his sister there waiting. She did her best to make him feel as if each new plan was his own, but he was no fool. He knew his puppet master well, and he needed her. Without Fia to guide him, he had no chance of destroying Arran Conall so that he could take over as laird and put a Kinnaird back in power over their territory.

She was talented at deceit and quick to think of each new step in their plan. He hoped today her ideas would be at their best. He had to find a way to rid himself of Edana for good.

"Aye, she told him last night, but his reaction was no what we had hoped. He was no so pleased to hear about his coming child."

Fia waved her hand dismissively in front of him. "'Tis no matter to us. Such news is difficult for any man when the woman carrying his child is no the one he loves. The newness will wear away. Soon he will fall in love with the child, real or no. Why do ye look so upset, brother? The wretch did as ye bid, did she no?"

"'Tis no enough to destroy Arran. I canna be with Edana. 'Tis time that we rid ourselves of her as well and find another way to ruin Arran." Tormod paced around the room, frustrated and tired of his act with Edana. Each time he saw her, she clung closer to him. His patience was growing thin.

"Nay, ye are too filled with haste. As long as Arran believes that Edana is carrying his child, she is of use to us. If we were to end her life now, Arran would no have the attachment to the thought of a child as he will in a few months. When it comes time for her pregnancy to show, we shall release ye from her so that Arran doesna find out that she wasna truly carrying his child."

Tormod could see the sense in her words, but it did nothing to ease his impatience. Still, he would have to spend the months until Edana's death imagining it, savoring each image of her slowly taking her last breath. "How will we kill her when the time comes?"

His sister turned to him slowly, a smile spreading across her thin face that sent chills down even his spine.

"I know a woman, a witch really. She has given me a poison that will kill her. When it comes time that Arran could see that she isna carrying his child, ye will give it to her and tell her that it is an herb that will make it appear as if she lost the child by starting a bleed. She willna know when she takes it that it shall kill her. When it is discovered that she is dead, it will look as if she died from an early labor with the child."

It would be perfect, far better than any plan Tormod could have devised on his own. Not only would the lass die in a way that would appear natural, but she would realize before she died that she'd been betrayed, that Tormod did not love her.

He could tolerate Edana a few months more. Then her perfectly tragic death would be the reward for his patience.

Chapter 26

After his conversation with Gara, Arran sat inside his bedchamber absorbed in his own thoughts of regret and self-pity. He knew it was wrong for him not to go to Edana, not to express to her how pleased he was that she was carrying his child, but he couldn't bring himself to lie to the lass once more.

Their marriage was a lie, the reasons Arran had married her invalid. For Edana was not the woman she'd made herself out to be while staying at Conall Castle. Not only that, but each time he'd taken her to his bed, he'd been dreaming of another, a lass so special to him that the only children he'd ever imagined himself having were hers.

He was a man torn, sworn by law and his marriage oath that he would stay by Edana's side, but promised by soul and heart to a lass who was waiting for him at his brother's home.

He'd yet to seek out Blaire, afraid that each moment spent together would only make the moments apart more difficult. And now with the news of his unborn child, he was afraid it would be impossible for him to go to Blaire without being crushed by the weight of his guilt.

If it were only Edana, his love for Blaire might have been enough to push away his feelings of guilt. But now with a child on the way, he knew he could not.

Arran would not allow himself to be the sort of man to teach his children that such behavior was acceptable. It was bad enough the way he'd treated women before, using them for his enjoyment and then discarding them before the heat from them had left his bed.

Blaire had changed him. He now could see the value of owning a woman's heart, the strength, responsibility, and the pure happy misery that came with possessing such a gift. He would teach his sons to view women the same way, but he would be unable to do so if he continued to dishonor their mother through his relationship with Blaire.

It didn't matter that he did not love his wife. His conscience didn't care. It would be the hardest thing he would ever have to do, to give up his heart so quickly after having it returned to him. But his child would need a parent who lived a life of honor, more so than most if the child's mother was to be Edana Kinnaird.

He would tell Blaire face-to-face. 'Twas the least he could do. His heart demanded that he see her one last time, to hold her and give her whatever explanation and apology he could offer. He knew nothing would be enough to heal the hurt he would cause her with his farewell. It had been she, after all, who'd tried to speak reason, saying that they could not meet again after their last night together.

He'd been a heedless fool. Unable to see the cards that fate would deal him, he'd promised Blaire he would come to her to claim her as his own as often as he could. Now he would have to break her heart all over again.

His heart heavy and his spirit broken, he sat down at his desk to pen a letter to her. He would tell her nothing of why he needed to see her, only that she meet him at the small cottage not far from

151

Conall Castle in one week's time. She would come, her smile illuminating the four walls in which he would meet her. That smile he would soon snuff out, the smile he was afraid once gone would send him plummeting into the darkness he'd once known so well.

* * *

Conall Castle

Several weeks had passed with no news from Arran. I found myself growing more certain that news would never come. I'd suspected as much when we'd said our goodbyes, but I hadna realized how miserable waiting for him would be.

Despite Arran's promise that we would see each other again, I knew what kind of men the Conall lads were. I knew the kind of man their father had been. It would no set well with Arran to have a mistress, regardless of the quality of his marriage.

Quality mattered not in this time anyway, as most marriages had little to do with the love of the people getting married. 'Twas one's ability to dissolve a marriage that was one of the things I'd found most fascinating about my time spent in the twenty-first century. If only Arran had married Edana there.

But he hadna, and such a wish could never be. So as I continued to tear the handful of herbs Mary had given me, tossing them into the stew as she stirred, I talked to ease my mind of thoughts of loneliness.

"What do ye think of Adelle and me father? Do ye think that if they spent more time together, they could get on well?" I already knew the answer, but I also knew the reaction such a question would garner from Mary, so I let it slip out innocently, trying no to grin as I waited for her overzealous response.

Instead of Mary, Adelle's voice answered from the doorway. "Oh gosh no, sweetheart. Your dad is a nice enough fellow, but truth be told, he looks so much like my ex-husband, it's hard for me to spend more than a few minutes in the same room with him."

I smiled and winked back at Adelle as I nudged me head toward Mary. "Aye, I know. I only wanted to hear Mary ramble on about how ye are no deserving of me father. If I dinna know better, I would say that Mary has taken a fancy to him herself."

Mary whacked the wooden spoon she was using to stir the stew hard against the table. "And what of it if I find him to be a fine looking man? There's no harm in looking at him when he passes by. I dare either one of ye to spend forty-five years married to Kip and see if ye doona find other lads pleasing to the eye. Kip does the same thing, and I'll no be one to deny him the pleasure of doing so."

Adelle walked around the table and tugged on the sleeve of my dress as if requesting that I accompany her. "Right you are, Mary. It's healthy to recognize beauty when you see it. I'd be lying if I said I wasn't green with envy over my daughter's new husband. They just simply stop making men like that within the next few centuries."

I laughed and brushed my hands against each other to rid themselves of the remaining pieces of herbs. "I'll be back shortly, Mary, to help plate the meal for supper."

Mary nodded and turned her attention back to the stew. "Aye, that will be fine, lass. Ye know that ye doona have to be down here cooking away with me anyway. I appreciate yer help."

Once we were outside the basement kitchen, I noticed the folded piece of parchment Adelle concealed in her hands. Flashing it before me, she waved it in the direction of the stairs. Grabbing a lantern outside the kitchen door, we walked halfway down the flight of stairs before stopping to sit down on the steps next to one another.

"This came for you this morning. I saw the messenger riding in and went to greet him before nosier eyes saw it."

I couldna repress an eye roll as I reached in the direction of the parchment. "As if ye are no the nosiest person in all of the keep, Adelle?"

"Well, I'll not disagree with you, but would you rather have Eoin gotten it? It's from Arran."

My heart thumped painfully at the mention of his name, and I found that my hands were shaking as I snatched his letter from her hand. "I suppose ye will be waiting until I share what's inside of it with ye?"

Adelle nodded and grinned widely. "What kind of a question is that? Of course I will be waiting."

It took me no time to read the contents of his letter. It contained only a few lines of his jagged script. "He wants me to meet him at a cottage he says is near the castle grounds. I doona believe I've been there before." I paused, unsure how to express how I truly felt over his request. "I doona know if I should go."

Adelle sat quietly a moment as if she were thinking over the best advice to give me. "Do you want to see him, Blaire?"

The words slipped out easily without hesitation. "Aye, o'course I do. I miss him every moment that I am no with him. But he is married, and I doona wish to make him break those vows."

Adelle reached over and squeezed my hand gently. "You are making him do nothing. Would you like to hear my opinion? I'll only give it if you wish it."

I nodded, enjoying the feeling of her hand around mine. I'd been small when my mother passed away, and Adelle was the closest thing I'd ever had to a mother. "Aye, I wish it greatly."

"I don't know how wise it would be for you to listen to an old, modern heathen like myself, so take what I have to say to you as you would a grain of salt. Relationships are far less black and white than some people wish to make them appear. There are some instances when life causes us to make decisions we wish we didn't have to make, but those things should not be used as an excuse to deny ourselves happiness. Arran's marriage to Edana was one of those decisions." She hesitated, seemingly unsure of how to say what she wanted. "Do you understand what I'm saying?"

"Perhaps. Ye believe I should meet him, aye?"

She nodded slowly, squeezing my hand more tightly before standing. "If you want to, then yes. Don't deny yourself moments of joy with the one you love. It is Arran's decision to make, and it seems he has made his by asking you to meet him. Guilt is a useless emotion. Do as your heart wishes. You will regret it when you're older if you do not."

She started back up the steps, leaving me alone in the stairwell as I called up to her. "Thank ye, Adelle. I'm no sure if ye helped me at all, but I appreciate yer words nonetheless."

Adelle stopped at the top step and laughed loudly. "I didn't imagine that I would help much. I'm not very good at advice. Ask Bri. She'll vouch to the truth in that. She was always more of a mother to me than I was to her. My point is, I regret the things that I didn't do more than the things I did. And believe me, I was a wild child in my younger years. There weren't many things that I didn't do."

With that, she turned and left. I continued to sit in the stairwell, allowing the candle inside the small lantern to burn away as I gripped tightly to Arran's written words.

Adelle was right. Even if it was the last night I could ever spend with him, I would regret no seeing him more than I would regret the guilt of our time spent in each other's arms. Besides, I'd promised him already. If he sent for me, I would come.

Chapter 27

Conall Cottage

I arrived at the cottage just before sunset knowing Arran would not arrive until after dark. The day after Arran's note had arrived at the castle, I'd ridden in search of the small cottage, finding it only a short distance in the direction of my father's castle. I couldna believe that I'd never seen it before during my many trips to Conall Castle as a small child, but Arran had chosen well. It was beautiful and secluded among the lush, steep hillsides.

I secured my horse and unloaded the basket of Mary's cooking that I'd stolen from the kitchen just before leaving the castle. Making my way inside the one-roomed cottage, I started a fire and dusted out the rarely used room as best I could. I spread the food out on the small wooden table and moved to try and catch a glimpse of my reflection from a sword that hung upon the wall when I heard hoofsteps approaching outside.

However my face and hair appeared, they would have to do. Taking a deep breath for courage, I stepped outside to greet him.

He was as beautiful as I'd ever seen him, his blonde hair and deep blue eyes striking as the last rays of light cast themselves upon him as he rode in. He smiled, but it was no the unrestrained smile of excitement that I'd expected. Tension etched his face. As he dismounted, I could sense that something was verra wrong. His desire to meet me was no for the reason I'd believed.

157

Suddenly embarrassed by the spread I'd laid out for us inside, I moved to block his entry into the cottage, no longer wishing for him to see what I'd brought for us. He dinna say hello as he moved toward me, but silently pulled me into his arms as I stood in the doorway of the cottage.

He held me tightly, no kissing me nor speaking as my head pressed snuggly against his chest. His hold frightened me. He clung to me as if he feared he would no ever see me again. "Arran." His name came out rather breathlessly. He was holding me that tight. "Are ye well? Are ye ill or injured? Ye are frightening me a little."

I turned my head to look up at him as he finally loosened his hold and moved his eyes down to me.

"Nay, lass, I am no ill or injured, and I dinna mean to frighten ye, but I am no so well either."

"Come inside. 'Tis getting cold." I was no longer worried about him seeing the food spread out for him. He was far too troubled to notice.

I held onto his hand as I led him inside. We both sat on the edge of the bed against the back wall of the room. I turned to him, taking both of his hands into mine, each moment of silence a warning that my heart was about to break once more. "What is it, Arran? Ye canna stay silent any longer, what has happened?"

* * *

He couldn't begin to know how to tell her what he must. The words lodged in his throat, content to stay there forever if his conscience would allow it. Once he said the words aloud, he would be forced to watch Blaire's heart break all over again, the same as he'd done to her the day she'd disappeared into another century.

158

He'd sworn that if he'd ever had her back, he would never let her go; that if it meant he would burn in hell, he would do so to be with her. But all of that was before his child, an innocent in all of his mistakes to whom he could not allow himself to be so selfish.

"May I kiss ye, lass? And then I will tell ye what I must, though I wish dearly that I dinna have to do so."

* * *

I nodded, but as his lips touched mine, the room grew only colder. Instead of the warmth that his touch always evoked in me, an icy winter spread down my every limb, snapping every branch of hope I'd held for this evening spent with him. This was a kiss of goodbye, and my body rebelled against it. I pulled away from him, shaking my head as tears threatened. "Nay, Arran. I willna allow ye to do what ye are about to. I canna lose ye once more."

He stood abruptly, running his hands over his face and through his hair as he often did when he was nervous. He'd done so ever since he was a child. "I'm so verra sorry, lass. Ye canna know how much it pains me."

I stood as well, anger suddenly replacing any sadness. I'd known that he would be unable to live with the guilt, but why had he no agreed with me when I'd warned him our last time together? It was cruel of him to allow me to hope, only to destroy it once more. How many times could one man break and heal a heart?

I moved in front of him, shoving him as roughly as I could in the chest, determined to express my frustration and pain in any way other than tears. "Doona ye dare apologize to me. Why did ye ask me to come here only to tell me that ye can no longer do this? Ye had to know that I would believe ye were asking me to come and be with ye as ye promised me that we would. Ye finally tupped me, and as ye have done to countless other women, no longer have use for me, is that it?"

I dinna believe that's what he was doing, but I hoped that the words would hurt him. Instead, they only angered him, and he reached out to grab me roughly by both arms.

"If ye believe that for one moment, ye are a mighty fool, Blaire. Perhaps I shouldna have asked ye to come here, but I couldna keep meself from seeing ye one last time."

I jerked out of his grasp. "Ye are a selfish bastard, Arran. What changed since I last saw ye? Ye should have told me then, after that night, that we couldna be together. I knew ye were too good of a man to allow yerself to do so while married to another."

"Edana is with child."

'Twas no what I'd thought he would say, and the shock of his words must have shown on my face for he quickly continued.

"I expect me face was quite similar to yers when she told me, lass. I havena touched Edana since I knew ye were back, but she says it happened shortly after our wedding."

I could think of little to say and slowly moved to sit down on the bed once more. "So that is why then? Ye can no longer do this for the sake of the child?"

"Aye, lass. I shall be a good man for me child, even if it shall break me own heart to do so, leaving me a shell of a man. If she wasna carrying my bairn, I swear to ye I would be buried inside of ye now and every moment that I could be for the rest of me life."

He sat down next to me on the bed, crawling into the middle of it as he pulled me into his arms. Silently, I lay with my head against his chest, savoring the last moments I would hold him in my arms. I couldna fault him for this. If he dinna act with honor now, he wouldna be the man who owned my heart.

"Can ye forgive me, lass?" He whispered the words into my hair as he gently kissed the top of my head.

"There is naught for me to forgive. Ye couldna have known I would return to ye, but I'll no lie to ye and tell ye that me heart is no shattered, and I'm mighty jealous of yer wee wench of a wife."

He shifted in surprise under me as he tilted my head up so that I was looking into his eyes. "Ye have nothing to be jealous of, love. 'Tis only ye that shall ever hold me heart."

I shook my head in disagreement. "Nay, ye are wrong. I'm no jealous of Edana, only that she carries yer child. If only we'd both no been so foolish, that was a task meant for me. And I willna be the only one to hold yer heart. The child she carries will and already does so now, or ye wouldna be here doing what ye have just done."

He couldna argue. He knew the truth in what I said. Instead, he simply held me close to him, rubbing my back as his lips lay on top of my hair.

Eventually, I fell asleep. When I awoke the next morning to the first rays of light shining into the crack of the doorway, he was gone.

Chapter 28

I wasna surprised to find that he'd gone sometime in the night, but it made the finality of his farewell all the more painful. As far as I knew, there was no rush for me to get back to the castle, so I spent the morning inside the cottage with my arms wrapped around my knees as I curled up in the bed and wept.

I wept for Arran and his foolish choices that had gotten us to this point, I wept for myself and my ignorance, and I wept so that once I gathered the strength to leave this place of refuge, so separated from anyone else, that I would no cry for Arran Conall ever again.

Midday, I rose and tidied things before splashing my face with the cold water from the washstand, scrubbing away any remnants of tears. The iciness of the water brought forth an idea. I quickly stepped outside to see if the weather would allow it. Summer was upon Scotland, and the weather, usually damp and cold, was now pleasant and tolerable. I twisted in my dress, missing the freedom the clothes in the twenty-first century had given me. Unfortunately, 'twas still many years before women would wear trousers.

I walked in a circle around the cottage to ensure my solitude as I set my mind to going to the sea. A place along the beach on the way back to Conall Castle was just as secluded as the cottage. It had been years since I'd swum in the ocean, no that I had done it verra many times anyway. The seawater was much too cold. But today, it seemed a good idea, the appropriate medicine for my tender heart.

The water would hurt at first, its icy touch like a thousand pinpricks on my porcelain skin, but the pain would quickly fade and a numbness would replace it, a numbness that I hoped would work its way into my heart.

Ensuring that everything inside the cottage was just as it had been before my arrival, I mounted my horse and set out for the sea.

*   *   *

As I'd expected, no one else enjoyed the shore. Although the waves were larger than I'd hoped, I wasna going to let it keep me from a swim. I stripped bare, leaving my dress and underclothes on a mossy rock as I descended into the shallowest part of the water.

Two grassy hillsides on either side separated an inlet of ocean from the vast openness of the rest of the sea. A secluded strip of water, perfect for my wintry dip.

The first touch of water was so shocking I was afraid I'd pull my foot away to find that my toes had fallen off, frozen by the water's tight grip on winter. The air outside might have begun to warm, but the ocean had yet to catch up to the changing of the seasons.

Intent on no changing my mind, I decided 'twas best to plunge right in, and I dove headfirst into the sea.

I'd expected the ocean depth to deepen quickly, but instead, my head cracked hard on a rock on the sea floor. As I pushed myself up to break the surface of the water, I reached up to touch my head and gasped as my hand came away covered in blood.

I could taste it dripping into my mouth. As I struggled to catch my breath from the coldness of the water, I could tell I was bleeding heavily. Before I could drag myself out of the water, the sky above me began to swirl. Darkness closed in around me.

* * *

The jostling of the horse caused me to open my eyes, but the effort that it took to do so sent such a pain travelling down my head and through my back, that I shut them quickly once more.

I was naked, I could tell by the feeling of the horse's hair upon my calves, but I was discreetly covered by a tartan that I recognized as that of the Conalls' guests. "Where are me clothes?"

The man cradling me in between his arms as he directed the horse answered softly, taking care that no loud noise would hurt my head further.

"I expect they are wherever ye left them, lass. I dinna take the time to look for them. Ye were bleeding something awful. I thought it best to get to ye before ye drowned or bled to death."

"Thank ye." The words sounded distant, as if it was no me that said them. Although I could see Conall Castle just up ahead, I closed my eyes as I drifted away once more.

* * *

The Castle Formerly Known as Kinnaird

He'd not actually been in the castle since he was a small child, but he remembered the hallways well, and he had no trouble finding Edana's bedchamber.

164

Everyone in the castle was asleep and, if the rumors in the village were true, Arran Conall had been away for days visiting his brother at Conall Castle. For this reason, he made his unexpected visit to Edana.

He knew Edana would be furious that Arran had gone and would assume that their plan to claim she was carrying Arran's child had not done as hoped and kept Arran close at her side. It seemed she was right, but Tormod could not allow her to believe so. She had to continue to feign the pregnancy so that she could ignorantly take the poison at just the right time.

He knocked softly on her door, not wanting to draw attention from elsewhere within the castle. There were many men on duty, and he'd been lucky to make it so far undetected. It took a moment for her to answer. He couldn't help the way he was sure his eyes widened at the sight of her.

Her eyes were red, glassy, and shone with being deep in her cups. The longer he spent time with her, the more he knew that the lass had more in common with her father than she realized.

She stepped out of the way, nearly tripping, and Tormod quickly stepped inside to help steady her. "What are ye doing, lass? 'Tis no appropriate for the lady of the castle to drink so much."

Edana set down on the edge of her bed and patted the cover to motion that he join her. "No one will know how I'm behaving. I am all alone here. Me husband doesna care that I carry his child. He still finds time to visit his whore."

Tormod sat next to her taking the goblet of ale from her hands. "Edana, ye are no really with his child."

"It doesna matter. The plan dinna work as ye hoped it would."

He forced himself to reach up and stroke her hair. At least tonight she would be too drunk to expect him to do anything else to

165

her. "Just give it time, lass. As time moves on, he will grow accustomed to the idea of a child, and he will love what he believes is growing inside of ye."

"And what will we do when he realizes that there is no child? Ye said that we would think of something, but I canna continue to do this if I doona know that there is a safe way out of it. He canna know that we lied to him."

Tormod nodded and pulled his hand away. "Aye, lass, I know. 'Tis why I've come to ye. I have acquired an herbal drink that will make ye bleed when the time comes that Arran grows suspicious. It will appear as if ye lost the child. Then he will never know that ye dinna tell him the truth. He will only be lost in the grief of his unborn child. He will then be at his weakest."

"So it will no do harm to me?"

He stood and helped move her up higher onto the bed so that he could settle her for the night. Her eyelids were starting to droop. He was thankful that he would not have to take her into his arms this evening. "Nay, lass. It will do no more harm to ye than ye've done to yerself this night. Now, rest. I believe Arran is due to return home tomorrow."

Once her eyes closed, he slipped out silently, grinning at how easily she'd accepted his lie.

Chapter 29

Conall Castle

"So you will stay then?" Bri and Adelle sat on either side of me, grinning. Mary stood at the end of the bed matching their expression as I gingerly nodded so as not to hurt my aching head.

It had been one week since I'd knocked myself unconscious during my ocean swim. While my head started to hurt less and the wound on the top of my head was healing, my chest began to worry me. It rattled with each breath, and I felt more ill each day. Everyone seemed so concerned with my head, that I'd yet had the chance to tell anyone how sick I truly began to feel.

"Aye. If ye will have me, I shall. I love me father, but I doona wish to return home with him. Have any of ye spoken to him about this? He willna be happy that I wish to stay here."

I watched as the three of them shared glances back and forth. Finally, Mary spoke up. "Aye, lass. He said that he would leave the decision to ye, but before ye make up yer mind, he has something else he wishes to speak to ye about. I believe he will be in shortly. 'Tis why we've come to ye now. We wished to ask ye to stay before he has a chance to ask ye what he wishes."

"And what is it that he wishes to ask me?" I meant to say more, but the rattling built so I swallowed hard to repress the cough that threatened to burst forth. I was being fussed over enough by the three ladies before me. I dinna see reason to cause them more worry.

Adelle rolled her eyes dramatically and stood as the scarlet sign of her frustration rushed over her face. "He made us promise we wouldn't say anything to you, but I told him I think he's a damned fool for even bringing it up to you."

"Mom." Bri's voice served as a warning as we all turned to see whose face was going to match the footsteps making their way to the doorway.

Baodan, Lady McMillan's eldest son and my watery savior, stepped inside the doorway, leaning his tall body into the wood frame. "Ach, excuse me. I dinna know that Blaire already had visitors. I shall take me leave and return at a later time."

"Oh, nonsense. We were all just leaving." Bri stood and smiled at me quickly before waving toward Adelle and Mary so that they would follow.

Adelle called back to me over her shoulder as they walked out of the room. "We'll be back this evening. I want to hear what you told your father."

I scooted back in the bed so that I could sit up straight. As Baodan approached me, he pulled his left hand out from behind his back holding my rumpled dress inside his large hands. "I will no disturb ye long, lass. I only wished to return this to ye. I made me way down to the shore this morning so I could retrieve it for ye. How are ye feeling?"

He extended the dress in my direction, and I took it, smiling at him in appreciation. "Thank ye. I feel much better. Me head only aches a little now." The cough that I'd held back earlier would no longer be repressed as I lost myself in a fit of painful coughing that caused my head to pound severely.

Baodan quickly moved beside me, placing one hand on my shoulder and another on my back to steady me. "There ye are, lass. Yer head may feel a wee bit better, but ye are no well, are ye? Have ye told anyone of this cough?"

I shook my head guiltily. "Nay, I havena. 'Tis nothing, I'm sure."

"'Tis no nothing, lass. Ye breathed in too much of the cold sea water, and ill ye are. I'll send for someone to see to ye."

He moved away from me, and I instinctively reached out to grab his hand to stop him. "Nay, please doona do so. If it gets worse, I shall tell them, but I doona want a fuss over nothing."

"As ye wish, lass, but please promise me that ye will stay abed and rest until 'tis gone. I wished to speak with ye further, but I'll leave ye be for a while. Ye look as if ye could use some sleep."

"Fine, I promise. What did ye wish to speak with me about?" My curiosity was piqued, but he was right. I was exhausted and the coughing had caused my head to ache dreadfully.

"'Tis no urgent that I speak to ye about it now. We have time to do so later." He smiled at the confused expression on my face and ducked his head as he retreated from the room.

'Twas the first time I'd actually spoken to Baodan alone, aside from the moment on the horse, but I wasna nearly conscious enough for that to constitute conversation. I found it hard to imagine what he seemed so keen to discuss with me.

I quickly drifted into a restless and short-lived sleep, stirring as I felt my father's lips lightly touch my forehead.

"Ye scared me badly, Blaire. When Baodan rode up with ye, yer head bleeding so fiercely, I thought for a moment I would lose ye. Ye are all I had after yer mother died. I canna bear the thought of losing ye as well."

169

I reached up to dash away a rogue tear running down his face, and he quickly grunted in embarrassment. "Ach, I am no a crying man, but a father's love for his children is enough to bring a man to his knees. How are ye feeling, love?"

"Better." I dinna say more, no trusting my chest to stay silent otherwise.

"I'm sure that Bri, Mary, and Adelle have already been to see ye. Did they tell ye what I've come to speak with ye about?"

"Nay, but Adelle seemed no too pleased about it."

Father rolled his eyes rather uncharacteristically. "Aye, I suppose she dinna. She's a strange lass, but I canna say that I doona like her. She's fiery like ye, Blaire. I am glad that she was there to take care of ye in yer time away."

I smiled. "Aye, me too. Now what is it, Father?" A small cough escaped, but I was able to hold it in so that it seemed as if I was only clearing my throat.

Intuitively, he stood and moved to the water basin to pour me some water. Once he returned to my side, he spoke. "Baodan has asked me for permission to marry ye."

I spit up all of the water in my mouth and lost myself in a fit of coughs. "What?" I struggled to get the word out in between loud rattles of my chest.

Worry creased Father's brow as he scooted in closer to me and cradled me as Baodan had done earlier. Eventually, the coughing subsided and father shook his head in dismay. "'Tis no good. It must be seen to, lass."

I dinna argue as I had done earlier. He was right. Each fit of coughing grew louder and lasted longer than the time before. "What did ye just tell me, Da?"

"He came to me a few days ago and asked permission to marry ye."

"Why would he do such a thing? Are ye sure that ye dinna arrange this? Ye did it once before. What did ye tell him?"

He took both of my hands in his own, stroking them tenderly. "Nay, lass, I did no such thing. I was wrong before to send ye here to wed Eoin, but please believe me, I only did it because I thought it best for ye."

"I know." And I did know. I was the most precious thing in the world to him. He just dinna know what to do with me.

"I dinna tell him aye, but I dinna tell him nay either. I told him the choice was yers, lass. I will no make such a decision for ye again."

That was at least some relief. "Thank ye. Ye doona think that I should do it, do ye, Father?"

He looked down and shrugged before looking back in my direction. "I doona know, lass, but I believe him to be a good man. What will ye do if ye doona marry? Ye are welcome to return home, but I doona believe that ye wish to do so. What is there for ye here? Ye were no meant to work in the house of the Conalls. Ye deserve a family and keep of yer own."

'Twas a fair question but one I'd given little thought to. "I doona know, Father. But I doona know the man, and I doona believe that I could ever love him."

"Ye canna know that for sure, lass. I dinna love yer mother at all when we married, but she was me very soul by the time she left this world. I willna advise ye what to do. Ye are a sharp lass and, in this, I shall let ye decide. All I ask is that ye think on it. Speak with him. Get to know him before the McMillans leave in three days time."

171

I nodded, unsure of what to say. Father could tell that I needed rest. He bent to kiss me once more. "I love ye, lass. Sleep now and think of it come morning."

Tucking the blankets around me and pouring me more water, he blew out the candles as he left, leaving me in the darkness. I lay awake for hours before sleep finally took me, all that he'd said turning over in my mind.

Chapter 30

"What's the matter, love? What have ye seen?"

Morna jumped at the sound of her husband's voice. Slowly she opened her eyes, pulling herself out of the dream. "Ach, Jerry. It doesna seem to matter how often I help them, they always find a pathway to trouble."

He sat with her, wrapping his frail and bony arms around her as she'd known he would, the supporter he'd always been for her. "Who, lass? What has happened?"

"Blaire is verra sick. I doona think that she will heal on her own. She needs modern medicine to keep her from dying. I believe Bri will look for a way to heal her. If I can only leave something in the spell room for her, she will find it without having to travel forward once more. It takes a toll on the body, and I doona think Bri should go through again."

"Why dinna ye say so, love? Give me what ye need to leave for her, and I shall go at once. I know that ye doona like to return to the castle. I'll go and be back in time for supper."

Morna stood and kissed her husband firmly on the mouth. "I knew there was a reason I married ye."

Leaving him smiling in the living room, she went in search of the antibiotics and all of the other medications needed to rid Blaire of the sickness that threatened her life.

* * *

1646

By the next morning, I was coughing up blood and my skin was so warm to the touch that sweat covered my body. I drifted in and out of sleep, delirious, nonsensical dreams dancing before my eyes.

When the visions stayed present while awake, I really began to worry. My vision constantly blurred. I could hardly register when someone was in the room with me or when water was being poured down my throat. I knew that someone stayed in my company, washing me, trying to get me to eat, changing out my sweaty clothes and bloodied cough rags, but I could hardly speak, I was so overcome with fever. And I couldna move without the aid of another.

Liquid built deep inside my lungs. I knew death was coming for me.

Each morning, Bri would come to dose me with the medicine, Advil, she'd brought back with her the last time she'd passed through the portal. It aided in breaking the fever only for a little while. With each passing day, the medicine seemed to burn off more quickly, and I found myself in delirium once more.

On the fourth morning, I knew it was time to say my goodbyes. Only one person demanded the forefront of my mind. After Bri came to administer the pills, I asked her to stay and help me in the few short moments when my fever would recede slightly.

She stayed by my side until I could think more clearly. Knowing I would no last long, I gave instructions right away. "Bri,

I need ye to get me some parchment and a pen. I need to write to Arran and tell him what is happening. I need him to come and say goodbye."

Bri started to argue but as she looked me over, decided against it. She too could tell that there was no much life left in me. I scribbled the note quickly, grimacing as a splatter of blood landed on the parchment as I coughed. I handed it over to her, and she sealed it without reading, respecting my privacy, as I'd known she would.

"Ye will send someone with it right away, aye?"

She nodded and placed a moist rag on my forehead. "Of course I will. Now rest. I'll take it to someone now."

"Thank ye." I shut my eyes as she left, feeling more peaceful than I had in days. Now I only had to hold on until Arran could come and bid me farewell.

*   *   *

Bri ran through the castle and out the back doors in search of Kip, calling out to him before she even reached the stables. "Kip, can you call one of the lads that helps you with the horses straight away? I need one of them to ride out toward Arran at once."

She slowed her pace as she rounded the corner into the stable to find Kip already ordering a young lad to mount up for the ride.

"O'course. He shall take good care of it. Won't ye, lad?"

The lad nodded, and Bri gratefully handed the parchment up to him, only pausing to kiss Kip lightly on the cheek before taking off at a full run back to the castle. Time for her to enter the spell room once more. She'd be damned before she let Blaire die.

Flying through the castle, Bri nearly slipped on the steps leading down into the castle's basement. She recovered quickly, not pausing to catch her breath until she stared open-mouthed into the contents of Morna's spell room.

Sitting on top of the spell book was everything they needed. Syringes filled with antibiotics, more Advil, and some medicine to break up the fluid in Blaire's chest all sitting on top of the faded, yellow parchment as if it had always been there.

She almost turned to stop the messenger but then decided it was best to let him go. These medicines would help greatly but, as sick as Blaire seemed to be, she didn't know for certain if they would be enough to save her. She wouldn't deny Blaire's last wish to see Arran if they did not.

Smiling, Bri moved into the spell room to gather up the treasures. Morna's days of magic had not ended with their last trip into the past. She was watching over the Conalls and her beloved home still, centuries away from them all.

* * *

The messenger rode fast, only stopping for a few hours of rest and to relieve himself when necessary. He'd seen the panic in the lady's eyes as she'd brought the parchment to him. He knew not what information Arran Conall needed so desperately, but his family had been loyal to the Conalls for decades. He would not be the first in his family to disappoint them.

He made the journey in half the time it would have taken most. Knowing his horse was in desperate need of rest, he stopped at the edge of the village and knocked on the stranger's door to see if he could pay for a stall for his horse while he attended to his duty.

*   *   *

The knock on the door surprised Tormod. Surely Edana would not be coming to see him at this time of day, and everyone else in the village knew better than to come to his home. He swung the door open to find a young lad, undoubtedly travel worn by the dirt on his face and clothing.

"What do ye want?" Tormod stared down at the young lad, hoping that his size alone would be enough to strike fear in the young man.

"Excuse me, sir. I'm travelling from Conall Keep and am on me way to deliver a message to yer laird. I was only hoping ye would allow me horse to rest here for a bit whilst I complete me task?"

"Conall Keep ye say? Let me see this note that ye carry." The boy backed away from him, and Tormod floundered for a better response. "I only want to make sure that ye come from where ye say, and then I shall return the letter to ye and allow yer horse to rest here."

Hesitation crossed the boy's face, but eventually he extended the parchment in his direction. Tormod snatched it out of the lad's hand before ripping it open to read its contents and then tossing the letter into the fire.

The boy lunged toward him, but Tormod caught him swiftly by the throat, pushing him into the side of his wall. "Now, lad, I suggest that ye get on yer horse and ride back to Conall Castle and tell whomever sent ye that ye delivered their message just as intended. Ye would no want them thinking that ye failed them, would ye?"

The boy shook uncontrollably under Tormod's heavy hands, and his face looked conflicted as he took in his words. "Aye, sir. Ye are right. If ye will only allow me to leave, I shall do as ye ask."

"O'course ye will, lad. Now get out of here and doona ever knock on me door again. Do ye understand?"

The lad nodded and fled quickly back onto his horse as he rode in the direction of Conall Castle. Tormod smiled ghoulishly as he shut the door to his home. Not only was Arran about to lose his wife and child, but his lover as well. And he would believe she died without him bidding her farewell.

Everything was beginning to lean in his favor.

Chapter 31

Two months had passed since the day Bri, Adelle, and Mary had come charging into my room and rather excitedly poked me in the bum with some sort of sharp instrument. That day and the days following, I'd been still too overcome with fever to question or worry about what it was they were doing to me, but eventually the fever broke for the last time and slowly but surely I was regaining my health.

Still, there was no doubt just how close to death I'd come. People still seemed nervous around me and avoided much conversation as if they were afraid I would break if touched or spoken to. I'd still no been allowed to leave my bedchamber. The closest to the outdoors I'd come were the few short moments each morning that someone helped me to sit in the window and feel the summer breeze.

I could really only remember the past few weeks, but I knew my days had been settled into the same routine for months. Mary would bring me meals throughout the day, staying with me to ensure that I finished all of it. Afterward she would spend time telling me stories as if I were a small child while combing my hair or rubbing my feet.

Each morning, my father would come to see me, but he would only stay a short while before heading out to help Eoin with whatever task he could. He would no return home until I was well, but he refused to be a guest in the Conalls' home without helping as much as he could.

The afternoons were spent with Bri and Adelle. It was my favorite time of day, for they were the only ones who seemed to have enough faith in Morna's medicines no to tip-toe around me in fear that any stress might cause me to die. They talked freely, and I usually ended up laughing so hard that the coughing would come back. That was when Mary would shoo them from the room.

I could tell by the angle of the light through the window that 'twas almost time for Bri and Adelle to arrive. As if summoned by magic, they appeared just as they crossed my mind.

"Hello, hello! You look much better today, hon. Time for you to get outside and stretch your legs, build your strength. It's certainly nice enough for you to do so, and you've spent so much time in bed. It's important for you to start re-building your muscle strength. I'm sure you're as weak as a new babe now. I think tomorrow one of us will get you outside." Adelle moved across the room to open the window wide, allowing the sunlight and fresh air to seep inside.

"I'll no argue with ye. Me legs have shriveled away to nothing. Come and sit with me."

Both ladies hiked up their dresses and sat with their legs crisscrossed on the end of the bed.

"Mom's right. You're looking much better. What did you think that first night I came and stuck that needle in your rear end?" Bri laughed and patted me lightly on the knee.

"I dinna know what ye were doing, but I was far too ill to care. Truthfully, I doona remember much of these past months. Only the past few weeks are clear to me."

Adelle fidgeted, and I could tell she had something she really wanted to say but dinna know if she should.

"What is it, Adelle? Please doona be like Mary and speak to me like I might die from real conversation."

Adelle laughed and stopped bouncing the bed with her jittery movements. "Fine. What have you decided about Baodan? You do remember your father speaking to you about him, right?"

I did remember, but hadna thought of it at all. "Aye, I do remember, but he hasna mentioned it again, and Baodan has never spoken of it. I know he's come to sit with me each evening the past few nights, but he doesna speak much of anything, and I'm no so keen to bring up his proposal."

Bri spoke this time. "Is that all you remember of your time with Baodan? Only the last few days?"

"Aye, is there more that I should remember? If there is, I am lost to it. The fever made everything a dream."

Bri stood and went to shut the door to my bedchamber so that we could go on with our conversation undisturbed. "Yes, but I'm not surprised that you don't remember it. Baodan has been at your side every day. When you were at your worst, it was he that swapped your bloodied rags and lifted you so that we could clean you and change your bedding. He wiped your cheeks with a wet cloth and brushed the hair out of your face, only leaving you when we instructed him that he must. It's only been since you've been more yourself that he's lessened his visits."

'Twas surprising to me that he'd done so, and I dinna understand his reasons. "Does he feel that much guilt over what happened, do ye think? 'Twas no his fault. I jumped into the water all on me own. If he'd no been there, I would've died that day."

"No, I don't think he feels guilty at all. I think he's quite taken with you, dear. I think perhaps I was wrong to react the way I did to your father's news of what he'd asked him." Adelle scrunched her face up in a childlike fashion meant to show her remorse.

"What are ye saying, Adelle? Ye believe that I should marry him? He's no even asked me himself. Perhaps, he's changed his mind."

"No, I'm not saying you should say yes. But just get to know him. See if anything is there. And I don't think he's changed his mind. I heard him asking Mary earlier if he could take you somewhere away from the castle tomorrow because he had something that he needed to ask you. Go with him and think about whatever he says to you. I think he's a good man. It's rare to see someone be so attentive, and he hardly knows you yet."

"Mom's right. He's been incredibly caring toward you, but Blaire, just know that you are welcome to stay here forever if you wish. Truly. Do not say yes to him because you feel that you have no other choice." She stood and motioned to her mother to do the same. "We should go, though. I expect he will be along shortly."

I called out to Bri, hoping to speak to her alone about the one thing that had hung at the edge of my mind even in the depths of my worst fevers. "Wait, Bri. Can I speak to ye a moment alone?"

"Of course." Bri stepped back inside, and Adelle waved at me before disappearing from the doorway. She sat down on the chair seated next to my bed and crossed her legs. "What's up?"

I hesitated, not wanting to show how much I cared but knowing that she would know as soon as I said the words. "Arran. Did he...did he come at all while I was ill?"

I knew she would no lie to me and, as I'd hoped, she played no games as she told me right away. "No he didn't, and he sent no letter back in response to what you sent him."

"Is it possible that he dinna receive it? Mayhap the messenger lost it along the way."

"No, I'm so sorry, but I spoke to the man I sent myself. He told me that he delivered it to Arran's hands directly. The man has no reason to lie."

"Aye, I suppose 'tis true. Thank ye, that's all I needed to know. If ye doona mind, I'd like to be alone now."

Bri stood and nodded once. "Absolutely. I'll see you in the morning. Get some rest."

She'd only just made it to the doorway when Baodan entered, and they passed each other on the way. He smiled at me but remained at the doorway. I was thankful it seemed he would no be staying long.

"I'm sorry that I dinna come to see ye earlier today. 'Tis only I've been working on something for ye. Do ye think ye would feel up to accompanying me somewhere tomorrow? We willna go far from the castle, and I've received Mary's blessing to get ye out of doors for awhile."

Images of Arran reading my note, learning that I was dying and choosing not to come to my side teased me, stabbing their way through my heart. He was truly gone from my life. I pushed away the pain as I smiled as brightly as I could at him. "Aye, I would like that verra much."

"I am verra pleased to hear it, lass. 'Til then."

He ducked under the door, and I rolled over so that I could stare into the setting sun. Perhaps the light would burn all images of Arran from my mind.

Chapter 32

"Nay, lass. I doona think 'tis a good idea for ye to strain yerself right before ye go outside. That will be hard enough for ye as 'tis." Mary lay the dress she'd picked out for me over the back of the chair next to my bed and pulled back the curtain so that the morning light would shine in.

"Do ye want me to scream for Adelle and Bri, or will ye oblige and help me yerself? I'm sure they would be more than happy to do it."

"Nay, lass. Please doona go hollering, ye will only get Adelle to do the same herself. If ye insist, I shall have a bath drawn for ye, and if ye wish to wear another dress I shall retrieve it."

I smiled triumphantly as I pushed myself upright and swung my shaky legs over the side of the bed. "I insist. I doona wish to be proposed to looking the mess that I do now. I can smell myself. It has been far too long since I've had more than a cloth bath."

"Aye, fine. I do agree that ye are smelling a wee bit like old cheese. Do ye have any other demands of me?"

Mary feigned annoyance, but I could tell she was happy to help and glad that I was feeling well enough to bathe. "Aye, can ye have Bri and Adelle come up anyway? I'd like Bri to pin up me hair, and Adelle willna like it if she is left out of the preparations."

"Aye, I suppose ye are right about that as well. Give me a moment, and I shall fetch them."

"No need. We're here. We saw Baodan this morning, and he told us you agreed to accompany him so we figured we would come and help you get ready."

Adelle came across the room to give me a light hug and help me to my feet as Bri smiled and extended a treasure in my direction.

"Look what I've brought for you! I went down into the spell room and got it from your pile of clothes. It will make you feel more human, and you'll like what it does to the way your dress looks."

"Aye, I know. It can work miracles." I reached for the bra and clung it tightly to my chest. "But do ye no think that he will notice it?"

Adelle laughed heartily, garnering a "lower yer voice before I thump ye" look from Mary. "If it was me accompanying Baodan today, then yes, he might. But I don't think you're the sort of girl to let a man pass a base on the first date."

"Base?" Mary and I said the word in unison, sending both Bri and Adelle into a fit of laughter.

"Never mind, dear. Let's start getting you cleaned up."

Adelle led me toward the tub as Mary directed the men who brought in the steaming pails of water. Before long, I was being tugged and pushed and prodded in different directions as all three women worked diligently to prepare me for the outing.

* * *

The Castle Formerly Known as Kinnaird

If Arran was counting right, he felt certain that Edana should have been swelling more beneath her clothes than she seemed to be. It was true that he was no expert in such matters, but it had been at least four and a half moons since he'd shared her bed, and he could still not see the slightest change in her physical appearance.

He'd also taken notice of how well she seemed to be feeling. She'd not been troubled by the bouts of ill stomach he knew many women suffered during their beginning stages. It had been bothering him for days, the wondering, and he knew he could not keep his questions inside any longer.

He reached across the table where they were eating their evening meal and laid his hand gently on her shoulder. "Edana. I wish to ask ye something, lass, but I doona want ye to be angry at the question."

She sat straight back in her chair, malice clear in her eyes. Each day he could sense her disdain for him a little more sharply.

"Why would ye think I should get angry? Are ye suggesting that I get angry often?"

There was no reason to be gentle with her. He knew that regardless of what he said, she would find a reason to be upset by it. "Aye. 'Tis exactly what I suggest. Ye stay angry all the time. Ye scream at people who have done naught but help ye, and I believe ye are a liar."

He watched as her face blanched, and something deep within him told him his suspicions were right.

"What do ye mean? What could I have lied to ye about?"

"I doona believe that ye are with child, Edana. Ye havena swollen at all, and it has been too long for ye no to have done so."

186

She stood from the table, and Arran could see that her hands shook with rage. "I canna believe that ye would insult me so. 'Tis only that ye canna see how I've grown with me clothes on. Kinnaird women never swell much with their children."

Arran stood as well, his confidence in his suspicion growing with every word she uttered. "Aye? Is that so, lass? Then, why doona ye take yer dress off for me right here and show me how yer belly grows?"

She stepped away from him as if she was afraid he would rip her dress right off of her. He couldn't deny he was tempted, but he was not the sort of man to disgrace a woman in such a way. Besides, he didn't need to. Her reaction was more than enough to make him certain she was not carrying his child.

"I'll do no such thing, ye wretched bastard. Do ye think ye can no touch me for months and then have me take me clothes off? I willna allow ye to do so. When yer child arrives, ye will see what an ignorant fool ye have been."

She turned from him, fleeing the castle, but he did not go after her as he sat down to finish his meal. She was right about one thing. He was a fool. A fool to believe his wretched bitch of a wife, and a fool to have denied the one woman who had really ever loved him when deep down, he had sensed that Edana had lied to him the night she'd come to him with news of their coming child.

Whatever misery a life with Edana would bring to him, tonight he felt as if he deserved every bit of it.

* * *

187

If it was the Conall messenger again, Tormod would kill him. Surely the lad wouldn't be so foolish to knock upon his door twice. 'Twas late, and night had long since settled over the village.

He opened the door and was nearly knocked to the floor as Edana threw her arms around him, weeping. "'Tis over, Tormod. Arran knows. He knows that I am no carrying his child."

He unwrapped her arms from his neck and pushed her away from him. "Slow down, lass. What do ye mean? Did ye tell him that?"

His face flushed red with anger at the thought. If she'd been so stupid, he would kill her this night. If she'd ruined their plan with her words, he would not put up with her a moment more.

"Nay, I dinna tell him anything, but he told me that he doesna believe that I am carrying his child. He has noticed that me belly hasna grown, and he thinks that I have lied to him."

He turned away from her to grab the glass bottle that he'd patiently held onto for months. "Then doona worry, lass. All is fine. If he suspects that ye are lying then it only means that now is the time for ye to take the herbs. Once he believes that ye have lost the child, he will blame himself for upsetting ye so. Here." He extended the bottle in her direction. "Take it tonight, lass, once ye are abed. Take every last drop. I shall see ye in a few days after all is done."

She wrapped her arms around him once more and kissed him quickly on the cheek. "Aye, I shall drink it as soon as I return to the castle. I love ye, Tormod."

He opened the door to show her outside. "Aye, lass, I know ye do."

Once she was gone, he shut the door to his home waiting until she was far enough ahead of him that he could follow her unnoticed. Tonight would be a wonderful night. Edana's death was finally upon him.

Chapter 33

Edana took her time getting back to the castle after obtaining the herbal solution from Tormod. She wandered the streets of her small village, the only home she'd ever known, with an inexplicable feeling of unease. 'Twas as if she was seeing the village and the people in it in a way she'd never seen them before, as if she were saying goodbye.

As a young girl, she'd taken after her mother. She'd had a sweet spirit and never understood why her father got angry when she would play with the children in the village. She couldn't see the difference between herself and the people that lived under their protection outside of the castle walls.

She'd had many friends. Her mother ensured it, taking her out daily to interact with the people of the village, doing her best to make sure that Edana understood how blessed she was to live a life in which things came easy to her.

If only her mother had lived, Edana suspected that she could have ended up being a better person than the woman she became. Her father had always been a terrible man, but her mother's death released him from his cage, and darkness descended over her own life after that point.

Never allowed to leave the castle and surrounded by the evil that seeped from her father, Edana could sense her soul begin to warp, her thinking begin to change as suddenly the people who had been her childhood friends seemed unworthy of her attention. For she was a Kinnaird, and there were few worthy of her.

Tonight she felt differently. As she passed the candlelit windows, she wished she could join the people behind them. To live a simple life free from the ghosts of her father was a dream Edana had long since stopped allowing herself to hope for.

But perhaps Tormod was right and once Arran was gone, she would be free. Together she and Tormod could create the simple life she longed for. He had to be right. Her trust in him was the only thing that kept her moving closer to the castle, even as a small voice in the back of her mind told her to smash the bottle onto the ground and flee from her life here.

Arran spoke the truth when he told her that she was easily angered, but it pained her to have it stated so plainly before her. She wished she could change, but she knew she could not. Her father's grip was tight inside her still, and words of anger and hate slipped off her tongue when words of kindness would not.

She was tired of not being the person she wanted to be. As she entered the castle and climbed the steps to her bedchamber, she vowed to herself that once Arran was gone she would put all of the past behind her and start anew.

Her bedchamber was empty as she knew it would be, but she felt uncomfortable at the unease she felt at finding it so. If Arran had somehow decided to wait for her there to speak with her, she would have been unable to take the herbal solution.

She sat the bottle down next to her bed as she undressed herself and donned her nightgown. Crawling into the bed, she propped the feather pillows up so that she could be sitting up partially in the bed. It would appear that she'd been in pain and forced to endure an early labor on her own.

Edana knew she would have to drink the contents of the bottle quickly so that she could stash it away, out of sight, before she began to bleed. Once she'd bled enough to raise alarm, she would scream for someone to come to her aide. She only hoped that it wouldn't be too painful.

Shaking, she reached for the glass bottle, wiggling the top off so that she could smell the contents. The smell was potent, and it made her stomach churn. It smelled nothing like any herbs she'd been around, but she was uneducated in such matters. There was no reason for her to believe that the mixture was anything other than what Tormod had told her.

Pinching her nose, she touched the bottle to her lips and quickly tilted it upward. She had to swallow hard and fast to keep from immediately retching out onto the bed. Once she'd drained its contents, she bent over to place the small bottle under the bed and resumed her position, legs spread wide apart, waiting for the bleeding to begin.

At first nothing happened and, other than the foul taste in her mouth, she thought perhaps that the process would be a painless one. But just as quickly as she'd begun to hope, a pain settled deep in her belly. She opened her mouth to scream only to find that nothing would come out.

The pain spread fast. Fire seared through every inch of her body. Holes burned through every vital organ. Sounds coming out of her mouth were inhuman, quiet as if her vocal chords melted from the touch of the poison.

She glanced down between her thighs to see blood draining out of her and knew. Poison. Not the herbal mixture Tormod had promised her.

Just as quickly as the pain had begun, it stopped. Her heart beat slowly in her ears. Her limbs hung lifeless and cold. Blood drained from her as she realized the mistakes she had made.

Her father's spirit never coaxed her to seek revenge on the Conalls. His spirit rooted for her own demise. The same black presence he'd been in her life, cheerfully led her to her death.

What a fool she'd been to believe Tormod. To believe that a man could love her and want to care for her. A man no better than her father.

The one soul who could give her all she needed was the one she was about to hurt the most.

Arran would not know that she'd done this to herself. That she'd lied. Once he found her, Edana knew Arran would blame himself and live with the guilt always. 'Twas no what he deserved. She'd been too foolish to see that before.

She took her last breath, praying that Arran would one day learn the truth.

Her prayer didn't include herself. She got no less than she deserved. Casting aside her hopes for a new life, Edana shut her eyes as death took her.

Chapter 34

Conall Castle

We'd all expected that Baodan was going to gather me for our outing sometime in the morning, but as the day passed with no sign of him, we quickly learned that we were no as sure of his plans as we thought.

I was ready before midday, all cleaned up, hair pinned back, and looking as presentable as I had in months with nowhere yet to go. The morning's preparations exhausted me. So shortly after I was ready and Bri, Adelle, and Mary were satisfied with my appearance, I lay down and fell quickly asleep.

It felt as if I'd only drifted for a few short moments, but when I awoke to the feeling of a hand lightly grabbing my own, I opened my eyes to see the light from the setting sun fading out my window.

"I'm sorry, lass. I should have been more specific as to when I planned to come for ye. I feel terrible that ye've spent the whole day waiting on me. Ye must be exhausted already."

I was but I sat up with as much life as I could manage, as I swung my feet over the bed and stood, only lightly shaky. "Nay, doona be sorry. I needed to get up and behave as a human for a while."

I was certain the back of my hair was a mess after sleeping on it most of the day, but I dinna want to fix it in front of him. What did it matter anyway? I had no real feelings for him, there was no reason to try and impress him.

"Are ye ready, lass? If ye doona feel like ye are ready to leave the castle for a bit, we doona have to do it. I wouldna like for ye to make yerself sick again by doing more than ye are ready to."

I reached up to grab his arm, the thought of spending one more moment in my bedchamber torturous. "Aye, I couldna be more ready to get outdoors for a while. I shall gladly go wherever ye wish to take me."

"That is me hope, lass."

His words made me nervous, and I instantly regretted my previous enthusiasm. I dinna want to make him believe I felt something I dinna. If he intended to ask me what everyone around me seemed to think he was going to, I had no answer for him.

I dinna know the man well enough to love him and, even if I grew to know him well, I was certain my heart was no capable of giving itself to another. Regardless of Bri's insistence that I was welcome to stay at the castle as long as I wished, I knew it wouldna be right to live a lifetime with them, relying on their charity and friendship.

And Father was right. Even if I couldna have the love that I longed for, I did still someday want children, a notion which before Arran I found repulsive. I used to think the idea of children a dreadful thing, but Arran's love had opened a part of me I hadna known existed, and even though he was gone from my life, those parts of my soul remained open.

Baodan held tightly onto my hand as he moved slowly down the steps of the castle, stopping to allow me to rest often, each step a struggle after being off of my feet for so long.

195

There was no question that Baodan was a good man. I knew Arran well enough to know that he would no have been as patient with me, and I dinna get the feeling that Baodan struggled with drink as Arran sometimes did. Baodan would be a good father. Perhaps if I did no want to be alone forever, Baodan would be a fine choice of a man to spend my life with.

I dinna yet know, but I set my mind to consider the possibility. I would listen to all he had to say and then hopefully, the right decision would come.

* * *

He'd lifted me onto his horse with ease. Whether I wanted to or no, I was forced to lean back against him. My muscles were so weak and tired, I was trembling terribly from the effort it had taken to just make it out of the castle.

My weak muscles were enough to make me shake, but within moments of leaving, I became certain I knew where we were headed. Not that he could have known. No way could he know of the memories this place would bring up for me, the pain that I had suffered here. No one at the castle, save Adelle, would have known that I'd been here before, and I was certain she dinna know that the cottage was where Baodan had planned to take me.

He'd been here today, readying it for this evening, as candles burned inside the windows. The entire place was alight with the soft glow of tiny flames.

Baodan pulled up next to the cottage, dismounting and then carefully helping me off the top of the horse. He continued to hold on to both of my elbows, to help me stay steady, as he led me inside.

196

"If I know the three lassies that spend every spare moment by yer side, I expect that ye already have some idea as to why I've brought ye here. But I doona wish to speak of that right away. First, I'd like simply to eat with ye and visit so that we may get to know one another a little more. Would that be acceptable to ye, lass?"

"Aye, it would." I sat down at the seat he pulled away from the table for me. I did my best to push away all memories I had of the last time I'd been here.

As soon as we sat down and started eating, Baodan spoke. "I know that I doona know ye well, lass, and ye doona know me either, but 'tis me ardent wish that we both grow to know each other better."

"Aye? Well, anything ye wish to know, I shall tell ye. Many think I am much too free with what I say." The food was delicious, and I relished in the enjoyment of eating at a table rather than in bed.

"I doona mind that at all in a lass. Me beloved wife was much the same way."

I certainly hadna suspected that of him. I hadna known that he'd been married once before and, while I knew him to be at least five years older than myself, he dinna look it at all. To imagine him with such a past was difficult.

"Aye? I dinna know that ye were married. What? How did she?" I was unsure of how to say what I meant to ask, but I was sure he would understand my meaning well enough.

"How did I lose her, lass? Six years ago, 'tis been. We'd only been married a year when the sickness came for her. I was away on a short trip, gone for only a fortnight to help a man with acquiring a piece of land. I knew not that she'd been ill until I returned home to find her dead. I live with the guilt of no being there with her those last days always."

That went a long ways toward explaining his attentiveness while I was so ill, and I felt uncomfortable at the thought that my stupidity had caused him to re-live such pain. "I'm verra sorry. I doona know what else to tell ye, save that."

He shook his head and took a deep breath, seemingly pushing his own dark memories away. "There is naught to say but that, but I appreciate yer kindness. I thought that ye should know before I ask ye what I intend. Yer father has spoken to ye of what I asked him, aye?"

I nodded, swallowing my mouthful of food and scooting my plate away so that I wouldna be tempted to eat more. "He has, but if ye intend to ask it, I'd prefer to hear it from ye as well."

He smiled and stood, dragging his chair so that it was in front of mine. He resumed his seat and gathered both of my hands in his. "Aye, lass, that would only be right of me, would it no? I shall ask ye what I asked yer father, but I wish to be honest with ye first, if ye would allow me to be so."

"O'course. I would wish nothing less than whatever truth ye have to give."

"I am no in love with ye, lass, and I doona know if I ever will be. Me heart was buried with me wife long ago, but that doesna mean that I doona want a family, and I doona wish to spend the rest of me days alone."

He paused and looked at me as if unsure if he should say what he wished to say next. "Go on. Say whatever ye wish, and I will no take offense to it." Truthfully, I was pleased that he dinna offer a confession of love. It would have been unkind of me to accept it when I had none that I could return to him.

"Verra well, lass. I've heard some talk that ye yerself have lost a love. Nay on purpose, but yer three bonny friends doona speak as quiet as they sometimes think they do. I've come to believe that perhaps yer heart is in much the same place as mine and that it belongs to another and always shall. There was one name that ye whispered during yer fevers over and over again, and I doona wish to cause ye pain by speaking it here."

My intake of breath was sharp, and he could see that he'd surprised me. "I dinna know that I'd done so. Bri, Adelle, and Mary never said."

"I know that ye dinna, lass, and I doubt that they were privy to seeing ye do so, as well. They were often with ye only when ye were awake. I was afraid to speak much with ye, so I kept ye company often while ye slept."

"Ah."

He laughed softly before continuing. "Perhaps, I should have kept that to meself, aye? That may be unsettling to ye, but I assure ye, lass, I was only watching over ye to make sure ye were safe and as comfortable as ye could be."

I squeezed his hand wrapped around my own. "Aye, I know. 'Tis a comfort to know I was so well watched after. Thank ye. I havena told ye thank ye enough for saving me life."

"I deserve no thanks, lass. Any man but the worst would have done the same. But this is really what I've brought ye here to ask of ye." He fidgeted nervously, and I rubbed my thumb back and forth across his hand to calm him. He smiled as he looked down at our entwined hands. "I believe that we are both of similar hearts and minds, lass. While I know that I canna give ye what ye once had, I can give ye companionship. And I swear to ye that I will offer ye protection and a happy home. As for any children that we may have together, I will love them and serve them for all of me days. Will ye marry me, Blaire?"

Arran was gone. Whether he was happy in his marriage or no, he was now expecting his own child. When he'd said goodbye to me the last time I was in this cottage, he'd certainly meant it. Even word that I might die was no enough to bring him back to my side.

Baodan was a better man than the one who owned my heart, and I wouldna be lucky enough to come by a better offer ever again. "Aye, lad. I'll marry ye."

He smiled as he leaned hesitantly forward, gently sealing my promise with a kiss.

Chapter 35

The Castle Formerly Known As Kinnaird

Arran woke in the middle of the night, his heart beating quickly, panicked and filled with a sense of dread. He rose, drenched in sweat, and paced around the room to try and calm his breathing.

He couldn't understand what would have caused him to feel this way. He was a sound sleeper, and he'd not been having nightmares. Just the opposite, actually. Blaire had come to him in his dreams as she did most nights. He delighted in the time he spent there holding her in his arms, claiming her over and over with his body. No matter how unreal or fleeting those moments were each night, he clung to them wishing each day away so that nighttime would come, and he could be with the woman he loved once more.

But tonight his dreams were interrupted. He could not shake the feeling that something was very terribly wrong. He dressed quickly, slowly opening the door to his bedchamber so that he could listen for any sign of trouble that might be brewing below stairs.

The castle was silent, dark, save for a few candles still burning. Reaching for the candle closest to him, he hesitantly made his way out into the hall. He knew not why he was headed in this direction, but every step forward brought him closer to Edana's bedchamber.

The lass should have been asleep long before now, and he knew he should not disturb her without reason, but something deep inside him lurched with fear as he stood before her door. He pressed his ear hard against the outside of the door hoping to hear her breathing or moving about.

When he heard nothing, he breathed deeply and quietly pushed open the door. He looked first not at the bed, but at the candles, still lit, scattered throughout the room. It was unlike her to leave them burning after she'd gone to bed. Perhaps she still had not returned to the castle. He knew he'd angered her greatly in the dining hall.

Slightly relieved, he stepped all the way inside and had to swallow hard to choke down the bile that rose in the back of his throat.

Her head lay oddly back against the pillow with the rest of her upper half propped up as if she were sitting. Her eyes were wide open and lifeless. Her legs were spread awkwardly open. It was then Arran noticed the blood slowly dripping off the end of the bed and the coverings drenched in her blood.

He screamed a deep, animalistic groan as the gruesome sight brought him to his knees in the doorway. He knew not how long he sat there, but eventually the castle began to stir. He was pulled to his feet by two servants but quickly jerked away from them as he fled the room and burst outside the castle doors.

With his first deep breath of the cool night air, he vomited as sobs overtook him. He knew it was his fault. The lass hadn't lied to him about the baby, and his screams and horrible accusations had caused her to lose the child and ultimately her own life as well.

How soon after he'd gone to bed had Edana fallen ill and begun to bleed all alone in her bedchamber? How long had she

202

suffered before dying? The questions that tormented him made him ill. No one, not even Edana, deserved to die such a death, all alone with no one to come and provide aid to her or answer her cries for help.

She must've screamed. How could one not when going through pain such as that which was so clearly etched forever on her face? If only he'd drunk less during their last meal together, perhaps he wouldn't have been sleeping so deeply not to hear her cries.

Arran knew he was not a good man. Not like his brother, not like his father. He'd battled demons of guilt and remorse for past decisions for much of his adult life, but nothing compared to this transgression for which he would now have to hold himself accountable.

He'd killed her. Whether it was by his own hand or not, he knew he would feel responsible for the lass's death and for the death of his unborn child for the rest of his life. Rising, he straightened himself, roughly brushing away his tears. The least he could do for her now was to see her properly laid to rest and beg God for forgiveness for all that he'd done.

Making his way back inside the castle, he began giving orders, stopping the castle's messenger as he passed him on the stairwell. "Ride for Conall Castle at once, lad. Speak only to me brother, Eoin, and let him know of what has passed here this night. He will wish to be here as we lay her to rest."

* * *

Tormod watched from his hiding place just on the edge of the castle gates. He'd left shortly after Edana, silently following behind her so that he could keep tight watch on the castle so he would know the instant his plan had succeeded.

203

It had taken longer than he'd expected. Eventually, he'd drifted as he crouched low to the ground, out of sight from anyone who would pass by him. Late into the night a cold breeze stirred him, and he looked up to see the castle slowly fill with light. He suspected then that someone had found Edana's dead body.

He hoped that was the case. He still wasn't sure if the lass would have the nerve to go through with the plan. She'd been quite shaken earlier when she knew that Arran suspected her lie.

It wasn't until he saw Arran's shadow burst through the castle doors and saw him retch all over the ground that he knew for certain the lass was dead.

He was finally free of the young, foolish, ignorant lass, and his soul smiled at the knowledge of it.

Tormod remained in his hiding spot watching the activity in the castle throughout the night, enjoying every moment of knowing how Arran would blame himself for her death, how just as his sister had predicted, he would be at his most weak and vulnerable in the weeks ahead.

There would be many in the village that would find Edana's sudden death surprising. Now, all Tormod had to do was plant the seed of suspicion as to the cause of her death. If he could bring the townspeople to turn on the new laird, it would go a long way toward ensuring his own place as laird once he did away with Arran once and for all.

He was so close to all that he wanted. Ridding himself of the wretched Edana was the hardest part. His sister would know just the right way to proceed to finish his task. Within a fortnight, he planned to be residing within the very castle he was lurking outside of now.

Chapter 36

Conall Castle

"So you said aye to him, love? And ye are at peace with yer decision?"

Father appeared in the doorway late in the night, shortly after we'd returned from the cottage. I'd just made my way to bed. It was clear that he'd waited up so that he could learn whatever answer I'd given him.

"Aye, Da, I did. 'Tis the answer ye hoped I would give him, is it no?"

He surprised me by shaking his head. "Nay, lass. I dinna wish for ye to say aye if 'twas no what ye wanted, but I canna deny that I am pleased that ye will be taken care of. Baodan is a good man. He will treat ye well."

I was so tired I could scarcely keep my eyes open, and I yawned wide, speaking to him in between deep breaths. "Aye, I believe that he will."

"Well, I'm happy for ye, lass. Baodan is anxious for ye to marry so that he can take ye away to yer new home up in the McMillan territory. If it pleases ye, I told him I'd like ye to be married at home."

"Aye, I would like that verra much."

"Good, lass. We shall all set out the day after tomorrow, the McMillans, the Conalls, and us. Sleep well, daughter."

He turned and left, and I chuckled lightly to myself. He was more pleased than he cared to let on to know that I was to be married, and he'd been quick to make the arrangements, no wanting me to run out on another wedding.

* * *

The Castle Formerly Known as Kinnaird

Gara waited until all of the other servants were to bed in the wee hours of the morning, after Edana's bedchamber had been cleaned and her body removed for burial preparation, to seek out Arran. She knew their new laird would not find sleep tonight.

She'd done as Tormod and Edana had bid her earlier for the sake of her family, but even she had not known the malice behind their plan. She'd gone to assist in the cleaning of Edana's room once she heard news of Edana's death, and as she'd bent to scrub the pool of blood off the floor, Gara had spotted the small bottle turned over on its side.

She'd picked it up, tucking it away as she tried to understand why the poor lass would've done something so vile to herself. It had taken her only a moment after she saw the source from where the blood had come to realize that Edana's death was not self-inflicted.

It was Tormod. The bastard had played Edana for a fool and she'd fallen for it, drinking the solution as he bid her. She must have thought it would feign the loss of the child so that Arran would not find out that she'd lied to him.

Gara's realization caused her to fear Tormod more than she already did. So she slipped the bottle away so that no one else would see it, but her guilt over the lie she'd told for them was becoming too much for her to bear. She could no longer allow Arran to believe her lie. If she couldn't bring herself to tell him the truth over the cause of Edana's death, the least she could do was to tell him the truth about the child.

* * *

At first he thought he'd imagined the knock at his door. The previous commotion throughout the castle had long since settled, and he'd assumed he was the only one still awake. When the soft rap began again, he moved from his stupor of self-loathing and guilt to see to who was at the door.

When he opened it to find Gara, he was certain she'd come to tell him what he already knew, that Edana's death was no one's fault but his own.

"I am verra sorry to disturb ye, sir, so late and especially on this night. May I speak to ye a moment?"

He stepped away to grant her entry. "Aye, o'course ye can. What is it, lass?"

"Before, sir. I lied to ye."

He was too tired to think of what the lass could have lied to him about. "What do ye mean, Gara?"

"The night Edana brought me to ye months ago, she was no carrying yer child, no that night. She was no with child tonight, either."

"What?" Her words hit him square in the chest, too much for his sleepy, guilty, grief-stricken mind to absorb.

"I'm telling ye that Edana lied to ye, sir. She was no expecting a child."

207

"If that's true, lass, how did she die?"

"I doona know, sir. Women sometimes do bleed unexpectedly. She just lost too much blood too quickly."

Arran paced around the room, unsure of how to take what the lass was telling him. He was hesitant to believe her even though he himself had questioned Edana for so long. "How can ye be certain that she was no with child?"

"I examined her meself. There was no child inside her, never was."

Relief washed over him. He was not pleased by Edana's death to be sure, but if what Gara told him this time was true, at least he could rest in the knowledge that it was not he that had caused it, and there had not been a child lost as well.

"Thank ye, lass. So when ye told me she had no threatened ye, I suppose ye lied about that as well, aye?"

"Aye. I could no risk her harming me children, sir, and we were in desperate need of the payment she gave me for me untruth. I apologize for any hurt I have caused ye."

"Doona worry, it was no yer fault. I'll no speak ill of the dead, but it was wrong of Edana to have ye do so. But before I let ye go..."

She stared at him hesitantly. "Aye?"

"Is there more ye know, lass?" Arran needed desperately to know all. "Anything else ye can share about why this has happened?"

Her eyes rounded wider as her head shook a denial. "Nothing at all," she whispered.

"Then ye may leave me now."

Gara quickly left him. As she did so, he sat alone in his bedchamber wrestling with his flurry of emotions. To go so quickly from overwhelming guilt and loss to possible relief and optimism at his future brought on a different sense of guilt.

He already knew that Edana was a horrible person and now after what he'd learned, it seemed he knew not just how horrible she truly was. Still, it felt wrong for him to be relieved at her death.

The lass had lied to him for some time. He couldn't deny knowing that had caused him to lose respect for her. But he would lay his wife to rest. Anyone deserved that much.

He was now free from a union that should never have been. As soon as he saw Edana laid peacefully to rest, he would ride to Conall Castle to retrieve his heart.

To retrieve Blaire.

Chapter 37

Conall Castle

The few days leading up to Edana's burial Arran had spent in solitude, silently making peace with her death and his regrettable decisions that had linked him to her. But now that he knew the truth of Edana's lies, he realized there was only so much responsibility he could take in what happened to her.

He would not allow himself to be haunted by Edana any longer. Once she was buried, he rode immediately for his home. He'd been surprised when Eoin had not come to him at the news of Edana's death, but he'd buried her quickly so he thought perhaps his brother simply hadn't had time. He could explain it all to him once he arrived back home.

Some of his new clansmen would question how he could move on so quickly, but he knew that anyone who'd spent any time in Edana's company or that of her father's would understand.

Arran couldn't wait to see Blaire, to run to her and beg her to come back to him now that they could truly be together as husband and wife and build the family they always wanted to have with one another.

Arran nudged his horse with the back of his heels as he saw the stables ahead of him. He was so close, only a few more moments and he would be able to hold her once more.

He rode into the stables at full speed, pulling up on the rein hard so that he could fling himself off the side of his horse. He hardly noticed Kip standing in the corner until he heard the old stable master's voice behind him.

"Arran, 'tis good to see ye, lad, but what brings ye here? The castle is empty save meself and a few other servants."

Arran walked toward Kip and clasped his dear friend on both shoulders. "Have they gone down to shoot arrows then?"

Confusion filled him as he watched Kip shake his head. Where else could everyone have gone? Not far surely. "Where can I find them then?"

"Slow down, lad. I'll ask ye again. Why have ye come here? I only just received word about yer wife three days past. I'm truly sorry, lad."

Kip's words brought back the sharp pain of Edana's death. No matter how he felt about her, he could not help but regret the loss of someone so young. If only she'd had the time, he thought perhaps she could've become a better person than she was when she died. "Ach, thank ye, Kip, but ye know as well as I that I should no have married her in the first place. 'Twas an awful mistake and one that I doona wish to repeat by allowing meself to spend one more moment apart from the lass I'm meant to marry. Where is she, Kip? Where's Blaire?"

Arran's nerves built as he watched Kip turn his face downward and awkwardly pick out the ground with his foot. Kip hesitated to tell him something, and it frightened him greatly. "What is it, Kip? Doona tell me that something has happened to her. Is she well? Ye must tell me at once."

"Nay, lad, naught has happened to the lass, but she isna here. She's at MacChristy Castle with the rest of yer family. She's set to marry yer cousin Baodan in two days."

"What? How could this happen?" Arran set to mount his horse, not wanting to stay a moment where Blaire was not.

"Well what do ye mean, lad? He asked her I suppose."

"So she doesna know of what's happened to Edana?" He turned the horse in the stables so that he could ride in the direction of MacChristy Castle.

"I doona know, lad. She may by now, but I was the only one here when the messenger arrived with the news. I sent him straight for MacChristy Castle to find Eoin. He is probably just arriving."

Arran spurred the horse forward, calling back to Kip over his shoulder. "Thank ye, Kip. I shall see ye soon. I doona intend on staying away from Conall Castle so long ever again."

* * *

MacChristy Castle

The messenger arrived in late evening on the day before I was to marry Baodan. I was away in my old bedchamber with Bri as she played with my hair, teasing it into different arrangements for the wedding when Adelle burst through the door, red-faced and breathless.

"Mom, what is it?"

Bri dropped the strands of my hair she was holding and rushed to her mother's side. I could tell that something was verra wrong, and I nervously twisted in my seat so that I could face her.

"Edana is dead. The man said her child tried to come early and both she and the baby have died."

The room suddenly felt much too small. As tears threatened, I stood to make me way outside, but Bri reached out and grabbed my hand to stop me. I dinna know what to think of Edana's death. I'd lived in jealousy of her for having Arran when I couldna and for carrying his child, but I wouldna have wished such a fate upon anyone.

"Blaire, are you all right?"

I nodded and pulled out of her grasp. "Aye, only sad. Arran doesna deserve such pain. Does Eoin know?"

Adelle nodded and turned to address Bri. "Yes, he plans to ride out in the morning. He shall miss the wedding, but he wishes to be at his brother's side."

"As he should. I'm going to go outside to sit in the garden awhile. I think it best I spend some time alone."

I dinna wait for either of them to respond. Holding back the tears as long as I could, they burst forth the moment I stepped out the back side of the castle and into the garden. I sat down on a splintered wooden bench, poorly crafted by my father when he was a young lad, and placed my head in my hands as I wept.

I dinna know for whom I cried, but the tears fell freely until I felt a strong hand touch my back. I'd been certain I was alone, and I'd heard no one approach. Brushing my closed eyes against my sleeve, I opened them and looked up right into the face of Arran.

Chapter 38

At first I thought I'd imagined him, too many nights of memories of him haunting me in my dreams finally come to torture me while I was awake. I leapt out of his gasp, staring open-mouthed as he spoke to me.

"Blaire, why are ye crying, lass?"

He moved forward to touch me, and I jerked away from him once more. "Doona touch me. Ye should no be here, Arran. 'Tis no true what I just heard about Edana and yer child?"

"Nay, only part of what ye heard was true. I'm here to tell ye the rest and to make sure that ye doona marry Baodan. Now tell me, why are ye crying?"

"Ye ask that as if I have naught to cry over." I couldna say just one thing I cried for, there were many. I was heartbroken for Arran's loss, I was heartbroken for myself, and I was angry that he would choose now to reappear in my life.

"Ye doona have reason anymore, lass. Now that Edana is gone, I am no longer married. Doona marry Baodan. Marry me, as ye are meant to."

Feelings of heartbreak disappeared, and disgust filled me at Arran's callousness over the death of his wife. I'd known that living with her wouldna be easy for him, but he was a man quite changed from the Arran I had once known and loved. "How can ye speak to me so when she hasna been dead a week? I know that ye

214

dinna love her, but ye disrespect us both by speaking of her so now and behaving as if I could rejoice in her death and claim ye as me own."

His brows pulled together, and I could see he was struggling with his words. "Forgive me, lass. I doona mean to sound so cold-hearted, but believe me there are things that ye doona know, and I wish to tell ye now. And ye know me well. I have no way about me with the right saying of words."

He sat down where he'd found me and motioned for me to do the same. Hesitantly, I did so, keeping some distance between us, for I knew all too well the power his touch wielded over me. "Then tell it, but I willna marry ye, Arran. I have promised meself to Baodan, and I shall marry him tomorrow."

He shook his head, unbothered by my words. "Nay, ye will do no such thing, lass. If I have to bind ye and carry ye off from here meself, I will do so, but ye willna be marrying anyone save me."

I dinna know what to say to that. Part of me wanted to kiss him and tell him how much I'd missed him, while the other part of me wanted to hit him over the head with something large and heavy. I decided to stay silent and wait for him to speak again.

It dinna take him long to oblige me. "Forgive me for sounding cold about Edana's death, but the lass was a wretched woman, and I canna claim that I am no glad to be free of her. She lied to me, lass. She was never carrying me child."

"Then how did she die?" 'Twas small relief to know that Arran hadna lost a child, but I knew that if he'd believed a child was coming, he would be pained to learn that one was not.

"I doona know for sure, lass, but I know that it was no fault of me own. I shouldna have married her, and I'll regret any pain I caused her always, but I willna be so foolish twice."

215

I reached out and patted his hand, only allowing it to linger for a moment. If this had been all, I would have followed him into marriage this very night, but that was no the case. Part of me was unwilling to forgive him. "I'm so sorry, Arran."

"Sorry for what, lass?"

"I'm sorry that me leaving caused ye to marry her. I'm sorry that she died. And I am sorry, but I canna marry ye now."

Again, he seemed no concerned with my denial of him. "Ach, lass, I know that ye doona wish to hurt Baodan, but he is a strong lad. He will find the lass that is meant for him. But ye, Blaire, ye are meant for me alone."

I stood, moving away from him, tears threatening once more. "Aye, once that was true, Arran. But Baodan is a better man than ye, and he was there for me when I needed him, when ye refused to come although I lay dying."

"Dying? I know naught what ye speak of, lass."

He was lying, I was sure of it, but the pained expression on his face dinna seem feigned. "How can ye say that ye doona know, Arran? I sent ye a letter when I believed I had only days to live, and Bri spoke to the messenger that delivered it straight into yer hands."

He moved too quickly for me to evade him and grabbed both my hands into his own as he pleaded before me. "Believe me, lass, this messenger dinna tell Bri the truth. Had I known that ye might die, no matter the cause, there is naught in this world that would keep me from ye. Tell me that ye believe me, Blaire. Ye possess every bit of me heart and soul. Had ye died, I would have as well. I willna wait to have ye as my wife a moment more."

He kissed me then, and I returned it before moving my lips to his ear so that I could whisper to him. "Aye, I believe ye. It hurt me

216

more than I care to tell ye when I thought that ye knew and dinna wish to come."

"Ach, lass."

He breathed heavily into my ear, his breath shaky. I could feel how much he longed for me. He gently pushed himself against me, and I gasped at the solid sensation against my dress. He dinna move against me further, instead pulling away to kiss me gently on the lips as he stared into my eyes, everything I'd ever wanted to hear from him evident in them.

"It pains me to know that ye could think it of me, but I know that I havena treated ye as I should. If ye will have me, lass, I shall spend the rest of me life making it up to ye."

"Aye, Arran, I'll marry ye." I kissed him briefly, moaning as Arran's hand on my lower back pulled me into him.

Suddenly, a voice to me left caused us both to grow still. "Will ye, lass? I doona believe that me wedding day will turn out as I'd hoped."

I turned to see Baodan standing not far from us. While his face gave none of his emotions away, his eyes, deep brown and beautiful, were sad. My heart filled with guilt as it broke for him.

Chapter 39

Arran left us, understanding that I needed a moment alone with Baodan to explain the best I could. I couldna tell if he was angry. Baodan was a man whose face was impenetrable, and I could sense that even if he was angry, it would take much to get him to express it.

"Baodan, I believe I need to speak with ye a moment." My words sounded foolish and obvious, but I knew not what to say, my face still flushed red with embarrassment and shame.

He surprised me by reaching for my hand and moved so that we walked through the small garden.

"Aye, that ye do, lass, but I doona think that ye have as much to explain as ye think ye do."

"What do ye mean?" I allowed him to lead me as we slowly made our way out of the garden, meandering through the castle grounds in the moonlight.

"He is the one, is he no, lass? The one who lay claim over yer heart even when he was no longer there? I knew there was someone, lass, but I dinna know it was me cousin."

"Aye, and I'm so verra sorry, Baodan. I wouldna have agreed to marry ye if I believed there was any way for Arran and me to be together. But now that there is, I canna marry ye. It wouldna be fair to ye for me to do so."

"Aye, I know that ye canna, lass. I wouldna wish for ye to."

I stopped my feet so that he would have to stop walking as well and turned so that I faced him, reaching out to grab his other hand as well. "Truly? Ye are no angry with me?"

He smiled, squeezing my hands gently. "Nay, lass. I am sad that I shall no share in the pleasure of yer company. I think that we could have been bonny friends, aye? But I canna be angry with ye for doing as yer heart bids. Ye are lucky, lass. Ye have been given the chance to be with the one ye thought that ye'd lost. If I was given the same opportunity, there is naught even the fiery pits of hell that could stop me. I am happy for ye, Blaire."

I hadna expected such a reaction, but after listening to him, I wasna surprised. He was the best of men. If I had more brains than heart, I would have married him rather than Arran. I stretched, having to stand on the farthest tip of my toes to reach him as I kissed him on the lips before pulling him into a hug. He squeezed me tight, and my feet came off the ground. Together we stayed there for only a moment.

Once he sat me back on the ground, I stepped away from him to walk back to the castle, but I turned to bid him one last farewell. "Goodbye, Baodan. Ye are a good man. There is someone else out there who ye will find that ye have enough of yer heart left to give to, and she in turn will heal what ye lost. There is no man more deserving of it than ye."

He shook his head shyly. "Nay, lass, I doona know about that. If such a time comes, I shall welcome it, but I willna expect it as I journey forward."

I turned away, silently throwing a prayer up to the heavens that love would find him, as I went in search of Bri, Mary, and Adelle. They wouldna be pleased with me if I kept all that had happened from them for long.

219

* * *

The castle had turned to pure commotion by the time I arrived back there after speaking with Baodan. Eoin, Mary, Bri, and Adelle were thrilled to see Arran and were all ready to resurrect Edana only to bury her again after they learned the lies she'd told him. Baodan's family was so angry with Arran and myself, I was certain a fight was about to erupt. Thankfully, Baodan showed up shortly after I arrived and calmed them down, taking them away so that they could make their preparations to return home.

All of the chaos ensued around me, but there was only one person's reaction I was concerned with as I made my way inside the castle. I spotted my father instantly, leaning casually against a doorway looking on at the screaming spectacle with ornery amusement.

He smiled as he spotted me, quickly pulling me into a side corridor before I could be swept away by the flurry of activity in the main hall. "So I hear that ye've changed yer mind on another wedding, have ye, lass? Please tell me that this one to Arran shall be yer last and that ye will truly marry him."

I laughed into his chest as I hugged him. "Aye, Father. If I doona, I shall let ye send me away to a convent."

"Doona tempt me, love. Now, let us leave this place. The two of ye can be married at the top of the river near here. It runs into a deep valley and is the prettiest place in all of Scotland. 'Tis where yer mother and I were married. If we leave now, ye can make it by morning."

We set out in the middle of the night—my father and I on our own horses and Arran and Adelle atop another. She was not an excellent rider, but she was no novice either. When Arran had told her she could ride with him if she wished, she'd jumped at the chance. I had a feeling it had more to do with her enjoying being in such close quarters with Arran's solid body than her no wanting to ride her own horse, but it dinna bother me a bit. I couldna blame her. Besides, it was I who would share his bed from this night onward.

* * *

By the time we arrived, the sun was just beginning to rise, casting beautiful shades of pink and yellow across the shimmering water that gently trickled down the valley, slicing beautiful curves into the green landscape.

The ceremony was short and simple, rather unlike the pathways it took to get us here. Adelle cried loudly throughout, garnering multiple looks of horror from my father. But at the ceremony's completion as we sealed our vows with a kiss, I dinna miss the small trickle that fell from Father's eyes as well.

Arran pulled me in close, running his fingers deep into my hair as he placed a trail of tiny kisses leading up to my ear. "I dinna think I would ever be able to call ye wife, but in me heart I always thought of ye as such."

I pulled his mouth away from my ear and brought his lips toward mine once more. Quickly saying our farewells, we left Father and Adelle to make their way back to MacChristy Castle alone. Mounting Arran's horse together, we set off down the valley, no knowing what direction we sought, and no caring as long as we were headed there together.

…And alone.

221

Chapter 40

Tormod waited until the group had split in two and each had departed, Arran and Blaire off toward the north and Laird MacChristy and some lass he knew not back toward MacChristy Castle. Only then did he crawl from his hiding space and walk far off to the west where he'd tied his horse.

Immediately after Edana's death, Tormod had gone into the village to spend time in the ale house in hopes that he would be able to spread suspicion of how Edana had met her death among the townspeople. His efforts had been fruitless.

All that he spoke to had lived under the miserable leadership of Ramsay Kinnaird and as a result were not as sympathetic as he'd hoped toward Edana and her untimely fate. They were also suspicious of him. Bastard or no, they still knew that Ramsay's blood pumped through him and were unlikely to trust him unless given real reason.

The people saw Arran and all of the Conalls as saviors who had finally delivered them from the all-powerful hold of his uncle. It had only taken him upsetting a small handful of villagers before he'd been run out of the ale house. They would not allow him to speak ill of their new laird or suggest that he'd done something so heinous.

He hadn't, of course, but the truth of Edana's death could never be known if he was to one day soon take over as laird.

Tormod had left the ale house angry and defeated. He spent the next few days sulking until he saw Arran ride from their territory in the direction of Conall Castle.

It didn't take him long to guess where or to whom Arran was riding. Tormod knew he was travelling to see his whore, anxious to fall into her arms now that he was rid of his wife. Not that he could blame him. He'd seen every inch of the lass the night he'd watched them make love in the barn, and there was no denying what a great beauty the lass was.

He knew not how Arran's new marriage to Blaire could contribute to his downfall, but he was sure that once he told his sister, she could figure out a way to turn it to their favor. He rode quickly, anxious to arrive home so that a plan could be made and a trap set before Arran and his new bride returned to their stolen castle.

* * *

"Ye are certain they are married? He dinna just go to take her to his bed?"

Tormod ground his teeth in frustration at his sister. She was smarter than he was he knew, but he was no fool. She often spoke to him as if he were a small child, not the man who would soon serve as her laird. "Aye, I wouldna have ridden so fast to ye if I wasna absolutely certain. I saw it with me own two eyes."

"Aye, good. Ye shall use his whore to turn the people against him."

"How? The people doona wish to hear talk against him, especially if it should come from either of us."

"Aye, 'twas foolish of ye to try and sway anyone yerself to begin with. All we need is to pay someone else to do our bidding as we did before. The people are too loyal to Arran and the Conalls, but they havena had as much interaction with the MacChristys. It will be easier for them to believe ill of Blaire if the news comes from someone that lives among them and they accept as part of the village. We are outsiders ye and I. Go and gather the midwife who confirmed Edana's lie to Arran. If she isna willing to help us, take her children."

* * *

Tormod reared back to kick in the door to Gara's home with as much force as he could muster. The small wooden shack was dark, and he hoped to scare them out of their beds. Surely when the lass saw him with his lit torch, ready to set her home ablaze, she would come with him willingly, and he would not be forced to take her beastly children.

He moved throughout the small space holding his torch in front of him, slowly realizing it was empty. Not only were Gara and her children not there, it was evident by the lack of personal belongings that they never planned to return.

Perhaps the lass had more brains than he'd realized. She'd not taken his threats idly. Still, he knew that his sister would not be pleased to know that they no longer had Gara under their control. But tonight was not the night for her to upset him. He was itching for violence. One day his sister would push him too far.

* * *

"What do ye mean, she is no there? God, how could ye be so daft, Tormod? To let her go after what she knows? I told ye that we should have disposed of her after she served her purpose the first time."

Tormod threw his fist hard against the doorway, his frustration at his sister reaching a point where he was afraid he could no longer control his anger at her. "Are ye no the one who suggested that we go to the lass and enlist her service now? I am tired of ye speaking to me as ye do! Ye doona know to whom ye speak. Soon, I will be laird of this territory. If ye doona wish to stay in the ruins in which we live now, you willna speak to me so ever again."

He blanched when she slapped him hard across the face, and his fists began to tremble as the world around him went away. All he could see was her screaming. He knew not what she said, only making out an occasional word as rage filled him. There had been too many years of her belittling him, of her ordering him about and behaving as if he was useless without her.

Fia might have been quicker to think of ideas, but Tormod always followed them through. Now he knew what he needed to do to bring down Arran. All he had to do was find another castle servant to whom he could coerce to do his bidding. He had no further need for his sister.

"Doona ye threaten me. Ye're a bastard. Ye were born a bastard, and a bastard ye shall stay. Any triumph that ye have ever seen has been owed to me. Ye are as useless as our horrid father and as daft as our mother."

As quickly as his rage had risen, an eerie sense of calm replaced it. Suddenly, it was all clear to him. Fia was no more than an obstacle, one that he could no longer allow to stand in his way.

"Goodbye, sister." He reached forward, grabbing her by the neck as he rammed the side of her head hard against the doorway. She was knocked unconscious at once, but he continued to ram her, over and over, until the gash at the side of her head opened wide, draining her quickly of blood.

He smiled as she died, stepping over her lifeless body as he went on his way to the castle. It would be easy to find someone willing to do as he bid, and if they would not, they would meet the same fate as Edana and his sister.

Chapter 41

Arran and I rode casually, no making haste to anywhere as we made our way deep into the valley following the river. We were both as happy as we'd ever been but equally as exhausted. Arran especially had gone days without sleep, and I could hear his soft snoring against my ear as I rode in front of him on the horse.

I laughed softly, just loud enough to wake him up and send him jerking upright in the saddle.

"I think 'tis time for us to take a rest, aye? If ye start to topple off the horse, I willna be able to keep ye from falling." I leaned back and turned my head to kiss him as he pulled up on the reins to slow the horse's pace.

Dismounting, he tied the horse to a tree. Hand-in-hand we made our way to the river. After searching for a few moments, we found the softest patch of earth and lay next to each other to rest our eyes for awhile.

I curled into the nook of his arm, imagining that while we intended to sleep Arran would first suggest that we partake of another enjoyable activity. But no sooner had I settled myself comfortably next to him than he was snoring loudly.

I reached up, lightly kissing his brow before I rested my head against him to try and sleep awhile myself, but I dinna drift long before I drew restless and stood to stretch. I would let him sleep as long as he needed. It was a beautiful summer day, and I'd taken a fancy to stick my feet into the running stream so that I could feel the water swish between my toes. My last experience with water briefly crossed my mind, but I dinna fear the river with Arran by my side.

The water was cold but it felt nice in contrast to the warm sun that beat down on my face. I leaned back, extending my neck to spread the warmth over me. I knew not how long I lay there, but I heard Arran approaching before I felt his hands on my shoulders.

"Ach, lass, ye look beautiful with yer bare feet splashing in the water and yer bare neck red from the sun. If I wasna a gentleman, I would take ye right here."

"Gentleman? Ha! Where might me husband be? I know not of this gentleman that ye speak of." I kept my back to him, smiling as he sat behind me and spread his legs, scooting close so that his front pressed flush against my back. His arms wrapped around my waist as he laced his fingers together, leaning in to lightly blow warm air into my ear and down my back.

I laughed at the sensation, squirming as he held me tight, tickling me with his warm breath.

"Doona move between me legs so, lass. Feel what ye do to me."

He thrust himself forward to prove his point, and I leaned into him. "Hmm...aye, there isna a way for me no to feel that, and what would ye wish to do with it?"

I smiled as I heard his breath catch. He hadna expected me to be so forward.

"Oh, doona tempt me so, lass. I took ye in the stables once. I willna treat ye like an animal again and have ye in the middle of nature for any passerby to see."

228

I wiggled my bum, intending for it to torture him so that he would change his mind. "I doona care if anyone sees. But look around, I think we are all alone save for the birds and fishes."

He disappointed me by bending his knees so that he could jump to his feet. "Nay, lass. Ye are me wife now. I want to honor ye in a bed with a roof above us. I willna take ye again until we have found shelter for the night."

I raised my toes out of the water, shaking them dry. Then I stood quickly making my way back to the horse. "Let's ride then, and I doona wish to make a slow go of it as we did this morning. I am no a patient lass, husband, and I'm anxious for this honoring that ye speak of. Where shall we stay this evening?"

He smiled, following suit as we made our way to the horse, him mounting first and then assisting me so that I sat in front of him, mimicking our positions by the river. "There is a small village nay far from here, and there is an inn where we will stay for the night. 'Tis a common place of rest for travelers so they doona often have rooms, but me father knew the owners well. They shall have a room for us, I am certain."

"Sounds lovely."

"Aye, lass, I shall be so sore from wanting ye that I fear we shall make all the tenants angry and jealous at our lovemaking. Everyone that sleeps in the inn tonight shall know me name, for they shall hear ye scream it over and over again."

"'Tis some promise, lad. I doona know if ye are up to the task." I smiled, squealing as he released the reins with one of his hands, gently pinching me bottom.

"Do ye no think so, lass? Well I shall prove ye wrong soon enough."

* * *

Arran was no a liar, and I couldna believe that we hadna been kicked out into the streets by the innkeepers and their tenants who were sure to be mighty angry by this point. But I'd also seen the payment he'd provided to the old couple. He'd certainly intended to assure that we wouldna be disturbed for the evening.

The first time he'd taken me roughly, and I'd had to slow his pace for I was certain I would be so sore he wouldna be able to touch me for a fortnight if he continued at the speed with which he'd begun.

He'd collapsed on top of me then and rolled me to my side, both of us trembling with the tremors that follow only the best kind of lovemaking. As we lay still connected together, sweat beading on both our brows, I was certain we'd fall asleep that way, remaining as one until morning.

I'd just begun to drift when he pulled himself out of me, nipping me playfully on the ear as he moved over me once more.

"What did I tell ye earlier, lass? I am no close to being finished with ye this night."

I smiled, bone weary and uncertain I could take another go if it was anything like what I'd just experienced. "Ye canna mean it, Arran. Ye havena slept an entire night in days, and ye have traveled a long way. I think that ye proved yer point well enough before."

"Aye, lass, I mean it. Nay, I dinna honor ye the way that I wish to."

I lifted my head just slightly off the pillow to kiss him. "Aye? And how do ye wish to honor me, then?"

"Slowly, lass. The first time in the stables and just now as well, they were no what ye deserve, though I daresay that ye enjoyed yerself well enough."

He smiled mischievously and I returned it, moaning slightly at the thought. "Aye, I canna say that I dinna."

"Good, I am pleased to hear it. Still, I moved too quickly, too overcome with me need for ye to take the time that ye deserve. I have been with many women, lass, and I know what each one of them desires."

I stiffened in his arms, no liking the direction he'd taken the conversation. "If ye wish to honor me, mayhap it would be best for ye no to tell me just how many women ye have treated thus. It does nothing to make me feel special, aye?"

He grinned, placing one finger across my lips to silence me. "Hush, lass. Ye dinna let me finish. I know what they want, but I have never given it to any of them."

"Ye are too sure of yerself, Arran. How can ye know what all women want?" I gasped as he slowly entered me once more, rocking gently as he closed his eyes and groaned with pleasure. He moved one of his hands down to my center, just above where he'd entered me and slowly built in me a sensation so overwhelming I could scarcely utter another word.

"What they want, lass, is to be worshiped, for a man to surrender himself to them, giving them every inch of his soul so that they know that once they've bedded him, he will nay love another for the rest of his days."

He paused to plunge in deep once more, and I cried out as he filled me, reaching up to pull on the shoulder-length strands of his hair. He kissed me thoroughly before speaking once more.

"It has been asked of me many times, in the way a lass would touch me, opening nay only her legs but her heart, begging me to give them that most precious part of meself. I always tucked it away, never understanding why I couldna let that part of meself go. Now I know."

"Aye?" The word came out breathlessly, extended as I moaned at the slow torture.

"Aye lass, 'twas for ye. Me heart waited for ye before I knew ye were to come into me life. I shall worship ye now, love, and as I do so, know that I share with ye me soul, for there is no other in me life but ye. If ye were nay to bed me again, ye would still own all that I am. For the truth is, lass, that ye've possessed me soul since the first moment I saw ye. By the end of this night, I shall lay claim over yers as well."

"Oh, Arran, doona ye not know by now that ye already do?"

The night faded away as he stayed true to his word and not a bit of me went unexplored as he worshiped me over and over again until finally we went to sleep, well after the next morning's sun had risen into the sky.

Chapter 42

"Now what did I tell ye, man?" Tormod stepped away, releasing the old man who'd served as gardener at the castle for three generations of Kinnairds, allowing him the chance to speak as he'd bid him.

"If I doona do what ye ask, ye shall kill me wife. Ye have her locked away and gagged her where I canna get to her."

Tormod whacked the trembling man hard across the face. "Nay, ye fool. I shall certainly do all that ye have said, but I intended for ye to tell me what ye are to say to the villagers after ye gather them together this evening. Are ye certain that they will come if ye send for them?

He glared at the old man, watching as he reached up to rub the side of his cheek now red from the impact of his palm. "Aye, sir. I know all in the village and all know me. They shall listen to whatever I have to say to them."

"Good and what is it exactly, man, that ye have to say?"

"That...that Blaire MacChristy is a witch. That I've seen her steal herbs from me garden so that she could cast her spells. That I believe she has bewitched Arran for some time, and it was she that killed Edana, no the loss of a child."

"And what will ye tell them of Arran, if they should find him innocent in Blaire's wrongdoing?"

"That the spell she cast on him is too strong and has addled his brain such that his bond to her will only be severed by death. That if we are to keep our village and children safe, we must rid ourselves of both Arran and his new bride, the MacChristy witch."

"Aye, man. Now doona ye forget what shall happen to ye if ye should waver in yer story. I will be in the crowd listening to yer every word. If ye should waver 'tis yer wife that shall suffer, slowly, and ye shall serve as witness to every horrible act of violence that I have planned for her."

Tears rolled down the old man's face, and they brightened Tormod's heart. Finally, he was the man he'd always hoped to be. People feared him. If his ancestors had taught him anything, it was that with fear came power.

He sent the man away to gather his clansmen. Tormod would follow the old man shortly, but first he had two bodies to dispose of. For come tomorrow, he would be laird. He would no longer have time for such trivial matters.

The first body was that of his sister. The second was the gardener's wife. He'd slit her throat only moments after he'd taken her.

The old fool knew not that he did Tormod's bidding for nothing. His wife was long dead, and as soon as he'd turned his clansmen against Arran and Blaire, he would join his wife in death.

* * *

We spent two more nights at the inn, leaving the room only when necessary. Eventually, we decided that it was time to return home where we hoped for nothing more than to have at least a fortnight of peaceful nothingness.

It took us mere moments as we neared the castle to know that we wouldna get our wish. It was night, but a large crowd gathered. We could hear the angry voices while still a good distance from the stables.

"What do ye think has happened, Arran?" Fear gripped me tight in the belly, and I fought back the urge to beg Arran to turn the horse around so that we could flee from here, something in the back of my mind warning me that the crowd awaited us.

"I doona know, lass, but I doona think there is need to worry."

His words meant to comfort, but tension hardened his body. Even the horse was hesitant to continue his march forward the closer we got to the village.

"I think ye are wrong, Arran. They've spotted us, and some of them are now headed in our direction. Perhaps we should leave."

"Nay, lass. I am laird of this keep now. Whatever has occurred, 'tis me duty to see to it and see that me people are taken care of. I'm sure that all they need is leadership to assist in what has occurred."

"Aye, I'm sure ye are right." I knew that he wasna, but I dinna wish to cause him to fear the approaching crowd any more than I knew he already did.

Slowly we approached. As soon as I heard the words they chanted, my blood ran cold.

"Witch. Witch. Witch." They screamed it over and over, fingers pointing at me with eyes filled with pity turned in Arran's direction.

"What is the meaning of this? Who among ye will step forward to tell me what has happened whilst I was away?"

An elderly man standing apart from the crowd hollered out, finger extended in me direction. "That be her, the witch. We should bind them at once."

I couldna make sense of what the man said, but I dinna miss the way he cast his eyes downward after he finished speaking, no looking up again as the crowd poured in around us. Two men stepped forward with chains, roughly dragging us off, chaining us before either of us had time to scream or protest.

Our mouths were gagged and our eyes covered as they led us away to somewhere deep below the castle. 'Twas no until we were thrown into cells that they removed our coverings, but it was too dark in the cell for me to see anything. I called out for Arran, feeling frantically around the darkness. "Arran! Arran, where are ye? What has happened?"

A voice that I had nay heard before teased me in the darkness. Malice dripped from the deep, unsettling tone, and I screamed as large hands gripped me hard by both arms.

"Arran is no here, lass, and I doona think that ye shall ever see him again."

Chapter 43

"There is no need for ye to do this, sister. Yer children need ye, and ye shall all be safe here if ye will only agree to stay."

Gara pulled her sister into a large embrace but shook her head, resigned to the decision she knew she must make. "Nay, I canna continue to live with the wrong that I've done. I lied once to provide for me children, and it resulted in the death of a lass who'd seen naught but heartache her whole life. I lied once more to protect them, but I canna be the mother they deserve if I am no willing to do what is right."

"But ye doona know for certain what Tormod plans. What do ye think ye shall be able to do to stop it?"

Gara didn't respond right away, squatting so that she could kiss each of her three children, holding them tight as she prayed it wouldn't be the last time she got to hold them in her arms.

"Go inside me dear ones, and be good for yer auntie whilst I am away. I love ye more than ye shall ever know."

She waited to sob until they were inside her sister's home, struggling to catch her breath. "I doona know what I shall do, but I know that I must try. I heard Tormod in the ale house doing his best to make the men believe that Arran killed Edana. He did no such thing, but Tormod willna rest until he has succeeded in turning me people against them. "Tis time that I share the truth with me clansmen."

"But ye must know that he shall kill ye if ye do so."

Gara nodded, pulling her cloak over her so that she could be on her way. "Aye, but I am no living now with the guilt tearing me into pieces. If I should die, at least me soul will be at peace knowing that I have made amends for the sin that I committed."

"God go with ye, sister."

Gara turned, fleeing into the night so that she would not be tempted to turn back and live as a coward. She could only hope that one day her children would know of her bravery and grow up to be the men and women she'd given her life to allow them to be.

* * *

Arran would not allow himself to lose her again. If he had to break his own legs and ribs to get out of his cell, he would find a way to save her. Any man that got in his way would find himself dead, clansmen or no.

He rammed his shoulder hard against the metal. If only he could get one of the bars loose, he could somehow squeeze his way out. It was so dark he could scarcely see, but a noise at the end of the hallway alerted him that he was no longer alone. He stilled instantly, patting himself down for anything he could use as a weapon.

"Sir, are ye down here? 'Tis Gara."

He could think of no reason for her to be down here. His first thought was that she must have been one of the ones to conspire against him. He knew that she'd already lied to him at least once before. Had she lied again when she said she knew nothing else?

But on second thought, he remembered that she'd come to him, risking her own safety to tell him the truth of Edana's lie about the child.

He called out to her, doing his best to be loud enough so that she could hear him, but restraining so that he would not draw attention from elsewhere in the dungeon. "Aye, lass. Do ye know why I was placed here?"

He listened as she made her way toward him. As she stepped into the small crack of moonlight beaming into his cell, he saw the fear on the lass' face and knew that she was not there to harm him.

"Aye. Tormod has convinced everyone that the lass ye are with is a witch and she killed Edana. He says she has ye under a mighty spell."

Anger boiled inside of Arran. He'd wanted to kill the bastard the moment he'd first laid eyes on him, able to see the lad's evil sprit through the hatred that shown in his eyes.

"Why would he do it? What does he have to gain from it?" Arran believed he knew the answer, but it was hard for him to imagine anyone wanting to be laird enough to go to such lengths. Ruling a keep was hard work and if he could go back, he would gladly give up his position as laird, but not to a man like Tormod.

"He wishes to be laird. He believes it is his right because he is the bastard son of Ramsay's brother."

"He is a bastard, no doubt, one that I intend to send deep down into the earth once I am free of this cell. Do ye know where they've taken Blaire? What does he intend to do to her?" His heart beat quickly at the thought of Blaire. If Tormod hurt her in any way, he would return whatever pain he inflicted on her, tenfold.

"Nay, sir. I doona know where she is, but the clansmen intend to kill her. That is clear from the mob that awaits ye outside."

Arran beat his fist hard against the stone wall, growling at the pain. "I am no so worried about the mob, all I can think of now is Blaire. I must get to her before Tormod causes her harm."

"That ye do, sir. I dinna tell ye the whole truth last time I spoke to ye. I was too afraid that Tormod would hurt me children, but now I have sent them safely away to be with me sister, and I have come to right the wrongs I have played a part in."

"What is it, lass? What dinna ye tell me last time we spoke?"

"Edana dinna die naturally. 'Twas poison that killed her, a poison Tormod instructed her to take. I doona believe that she knew it would kill her. I believe she thought it would only mimic an early birth and the loss of a child."

Arran shook his head in the darkness, disgust rising in the form of bile in the back of his throat. "How could anyone be so evil? Do ye know of a way to get me out of here, lass? 'Tis urgent that I do so before Tormod can cause harm to anyone else."

"Aye, sir. I have worked in the castle most of me life, I knew where a set of keys was hidden."

Arran breathed in a deep sigh of relief as he watched Gara pull the keys out from under her dress and begin to work on his lock. Once he was free, he pulled her into an embrace, quickly pulling away as he took off in the direction of the other cell block.

Chapter 44

I dinna know the man who held on tightly to me in the darkness. He pushed me back hard into the side of the cell wall and growled a sound so inhuman that the evil in it caused me to shiver uncontrollably. I was certain that my life was about to end.

A sound in the distance caused him to pull away from me, and I had to swallow to keep from emptying my stomach onto the cell floor.

"I did as ye bid me. Now, tell me where I can find me wife."

The voice sounded old and frightened, and I knew that whatever he asked of the creature next to me, he would not receive what he hoped for.

The stranger spoke, calling the man to approach him. "Come here, gardener, and I shall tell ye where ye can find yer wife."

Me eyes slowly opened themselves to the darkness, and I could see the outline of the man approach the cell. I also saw the glint of metal as my captor pulled the knife from his boot. I charged him, jumping on his back as I brought my fist down on the top of his head with as much strength as I could.

The beast was too strong. While it caused him to shift his arm so that his blow to the man wasna fatal, the dirk still slipped easily into the old man's side. I screamed loudly, hoping for anyone to hear me and come to my aid, for I knew that the dirk would be headed in my direction next.

My captor was on me in an instant as he grabbed my throat with one hand and pinned both of my wrists above my head with the other. I could hear footsteps headed in our direction, but it dinna seem the choker could make out the sound. His face contorted with rage as he did his best to squeeze the life out of me.

He was succeeding. As my vision faded, I was unsure if it was truly Arran that I saw reach to grab the dagger out of the man's side before charging through the open cell to send the dagger deep into my assailant's neck.

He released his hold on me instantly, and I sank to my knees, desperate to catch a breath as the blood from the man's neck continued to spray over me. I retched at the taste of his blood as it dripped into my mouth and I stepped away, no wishing to be near him as he took his last breath.

His eyes remained open, the same evil expression forever plastered on his face. Even in death, the beast beneath the man shown through.

It took me a moment to catch my breath and, by the time my head cleared, I could see Arran and a woman I'd never seen bent over the elderly man who gasped painfully at the knife wound in his side.

"Doona worry, lad. We shall get ye the care that ye need. Only hold on a moment more, and we shall find someone to tend to ye."

I watched as the man reached out to grab Arran's arm, preventing him from going for help. "Nay, lass. If ye leave here before the clan knows the truth, they shall murder ye on the spot. I am no long for this world, and I doona wish to be either. I see now that Tormod killed me wife before I even agreed to do as he asked. There is no place in this world for me if she is no here at me side."

242

Arran shook his head, intent on helping the man. "Nay, lad. Ye shall live many years still."

The woman to the other side shook her head interrupting him. "I'm verra sorry, but ye are wrong, sir. The old man is right. He has only a few moments left, and there is naught that we can do to help him."

I dinna know the elder, but tears sprang up in my eyes. If he hadna arrived when he had, it would be me lying on the cell floor dead. This man had saved me life.

"Aye, I told ye, lad. I know that I am dying, and I doona wish for it to be any other way. At least help me to fix the wrong I've done to ye. Ye and yer lady must stay hidden until the people have heard what I have to say. Gara, will ye help me to me feet and let me lean against ye so that together we can address them? Once we have both spoken, ye will be free to leave here, and I will die knowing that I dinna let the bastard win."

I could see that Arran knew he wouldna change the old man's mind. He rose from his knees, pulling the man up with him so that he could situate him on Gara's shoulders. He helped them to the doorway. Sending them out on their own, he returned to my side.

"God, lass, I thought I had lost ye."

"And I ye." I threw myself into his arms, sobbing as he reached to wipe the blood from my face.

A sudden hush outside the dungeon told us that our saviors now had the attention of the crowd. Hand-in-hand we moved to the doorway and hid in the shadows as we watched them inform the crowd of all Tormod's evildoings.

The clansmen were no surprised and, once the truth was known, the crowd gathered in close around the gardener, no longer in anger but to comfort their friend as he took his last breaths.

Arran and I remained hidden in the shadows, leaving the village to grieve their friend and hero. Gara came to us as they led the old man away for burial. Relief etched her face. I could tell then that she'd risked her own life for us as well, no knowing if she would come out of it alive.

"Thank ye, Gara. We owe ye a debt that we can never repay." Arran clasped the woman's shoulder, unsure of how to express his gratitude.

"Ye owe me nothing. I am more fortunate than I thought possible. Me conscience is now clear of the wrong I did ye, and I will return to me children when I dinna believe I would ever be able to do so. If ye follow this pathway through the dungeon, it will lead ye back into the castle where ye can clean yerselves and rest away from everyone. Now, excuse me, I have bairns that I need to gather in me arms."

Once she was gone, we silently made our way through the dungeons, no stopping until we were inside the castle. We knew that we wouldna sleep at all. We were both eager to await the sun, for it was the only way this day would truly feel over.

Chapter 45

"Are ye sure that ye are fine with this, Arran? For if this is something that ye want, I will stand by yer side. I know that there are many dark memories in this place, but I believe that we could make new ones here." I walked up behind him as he finished penning his letter detailing to his clansmen why he was to step down as laird.

"Aye, lass, I doona doubt that we could, but I doona wish to. This is no our home, and these people are no our people."

"They did accept you at first, did they no?"

He twisted in his seat wrapping his arms around me as he buried his head in my breasts. "Aye, lass, they did, but they turned on me rather quickly, as well. I dinna wish to be laird to begin with. I rushed into it foolhardily because I believed that I was helping another. If only I could have seen all the trouble that decision would cause us."

I kissed the top of his head. "There is no sense in thinking that way. No one can know just where their decisions will take them. All we can do now is make the best of our future."

"Is this decision pleasing to ye as well, lass? I wish to please ye and, if ye wish to stay, I shall."

I shook my head, unable to repress the shiver that traveled through me at the thought. He squeezed me tightly in understanding. "Nay, I doona wish to stay. I wish to return to

Conall Castle to live in the happy chaos with yer brother, Mary, Bri, and Adelle. And then, when it is time that me father can no longer serve as laird, ye can replace him. But for now, let us live more simply, with no of the responsibilities and troubles that come with a lairdship."

Arran stood, sealing his letter and slipping it away to give to Gara. She would be sure to share it with the clan, who in time would find a laird from within their own group of men.

The people wouldna be surprised to learn of our decision to leave. Few would approach us still, their guilt from their accusations toward us making them hesitant to speak.

"Ach, lass, ye are a mind reader I'm sure, for there is nothing that I wish to do more than all that ye have just said. Come, let us leave this place."

* * *

Arran was not deserving of the blessings given to him, of nothing he'd ever been more certain. Many men better than he were more deserving of Blaire and her love, but he would gladly spend the rest of his life trying to make himself worthy of her.

She'd healed him from a broken spirit, forgiven him of his wrongs again and again, and shown him the value that comes with finding someone with whom to share all of life's struggles.

He leaned forward to smell her hair as she rode before him, and he shifted uncomfortably atop the horse at the feeling she immediately evoked in him. 'Twas stunning to him how even looking at her could make him hard and ready to take her. He couldn't wait to fill her with his children. As soon as they returned

246

to Conall Castle, he planned to immediately begin work on that task.

Or mayhap, even better, he would begin tonight as they stopped at the McMillans to rest on their journey home.

* * *

We took the long route back to Conall Castle and, much to my dismay, Arran had insisted that we stop at the McMillans on our way home. Baodan was Arran's favorite cousin, and he'd no had the chance to make peace with him the night Baodan had found us together in the garden.

'Twas no Baodan I worried about seeing, but I knew that his mother wouldna want to welcome me with open arms. 'Twas a happy coincidence to find that she was away when we arrived. It allowed us to spend a happy evening with Baodan and his brothers, all of whom I was certain would become dear friends.

The next morning we set off early, determined to make it back to Conall Castle within two more nights. I'd settled comfortably in my seat in front of Arran, nearly falling asleep as I leaned back against his shoulder, when an odd flash of red caught my attention out of the corner of my eye.

I sat up so quickly, my heels unintentionally went hard into the side of the horse, and Arran had to pull hard at the reins to get him back under control. "What is it, lass? Ye nearly scared the poor beast to death."

"Did ye no see that woman, Arran? In the pond?"

Arran pulled back so that the horse came to a stop, and he twisted to look back on the pond that sat just at the edge of McMillan Castle. "Nay, lass, I doona see anyone. Ye saw a woman, ye say? Perhaps, someone is only taking a dip. Twould be a nice morning for it, would ye no agree?"

I shook my head, the notion was mad. "Never mind. I must have dozed for a moment and dreamed something strange."

Arran slowly nudged the horse forward once more. "Nay, lass. Ye werena asleep, I can always tell by yer breathing when ye are. Tell me. Who did ye think ye saw?"

"'Tisna possible, but the woman looked just like a lass I met in the twenty-first century. A dear friend of Bri's."

"Aye? Well I will tell ye, that does sound mighty strange, but tis no so impossible either."

He was kind enough nay to call me mad, but I wasna eager to discuss it with him further. "Aye, 'tis strange. Doona mind me, I am only over-tired." I nudged him playfully in the ribs. "I canna ever sleep, the way ye keep me up at night."

He laughed into my ear, and I smiled, the imaginary figure quickly disappearing from my mind. "Ach, lass. I willna apologize for keeping ye awake, and ye may as well get used to it for I plan to fill yer nights with things other than sleep for all of our nights together."

"Oh, I truly hope so, love."

He kissed the back of my head and tightened his grip around me as we rode toward Conall Castle—to our home, where we would finally be able to build a future together.

Epilogue

The Roadside Inn – Present Day

"Jerry, 'tis time for us to make ready once more." Morna stood, stretching after her dream as she smiled wide. It would be fun to tweak her spells, and necessary if the new lass was to cross paths with the one she was meant to.

"O'course, love. What have ye seen?"

"We need to make our home visible once more, but it shall be different from the times before. The redhead is headed our way." She smiled, knowing Jerry would be pleased. He loved company, and he'd taken a liking to the fiery lass who'd come so valiantly in search of her friend.

"Ah, 'tis verra good news, but why should this be different? Do ye no think that the lass will stumble across the spell on her own? Bri and Blaire managed quite nicely."

Morna shook her head. It was unlike any dream she'd had before, but she was certain as to its meaning. "Nay, 'tis no that. The lass will find the spell, but she canna use the same one that's been used before. For while me spell room shall be her portal, it doesna need to be her destination."

"How do ye know?"

"Because one of our lassies has already caught sight of the lass elsewhere, even before she's actually arrived. It seems that a force more powerful than meself sees fit to warn the Conalls of the girl's arrival."

Read all the books in Morna's Legacy Series:

About The Author

Bethany Claire is the author of the Scottish, time travel romance novels Love Beyond Time, Love Beyond Reason, A Conall Christmas—Novella, Love Beyond Hope, Love Beyond Measure, In Due Time—A Novella, and other titles. She grew up in the Texas Panhandle.

Connect With Me Online

If you enjoyed reading *Love Beyond Compare,* I would appreciate it if you would help others enjoy this book, too.

Recommend it. Help other readers find this book by recommending it to friends, readers' groups and discussion boards.

Review it. Please tell other readers why you like this book by reviewing it at the retailer of your choice. If you do write a review, please send me an email to bclaire@bethanyclaire.com so I can thank you with a personal email, or you can visit my website at http://www.bethanyclaire.com

Join the Bethany Claire Newsletter!

Sign up for my newsletter to receive up-to-date information of books, new releases, events, and promotions.

Acknowledgements

I'm finding that it was much easier to write down all of the many thank-yous for the first novel than it is for the second. So many of the people who contributed to the first have also helped in the creation of this novel. Still, there are some who simply cannot be thanked enough

Mom, you are the ultimate wingman. Thanks for the countless hours you've put in, helping me navigate this wide learning curve. I will never be able to repay you for all you've given me, but I can't wait until the day that I can at least add you to the payroll.

Maegan, for the inspiration and the subtle ways your personality has worked its way into Blaire's. Your quiet spunkiness and rock-solid hard head are just a few of the many things I admire most in you.

Dad and Montana, for reading the first book and hopping on the romance train when I never thought you would.

Charlie and Flag, my feet would feel bare without them there.

DeWanna Pace, your suggestions are always appreciated.

Lastly, to my other team members: xuni.com and Damonza.com.

Made in the USA
San Bernardino, CA
14 October 2015